My Crazy Blind Date Blog

By Ann Stang

Thank you to my family and friends who have inspired me. David, Rebekah, Jenny, and Kelli for your many excellent suggestions. Rebekah, once again for a wonderful cover. And Kelli, for brainstorming the ideas with me.

May this, as always, be for the glory of God.

Chapter One

I used to think a blind date was the romantic equivalent of walking down a dead end street with an open manhole ahead... blindfolded. If you'd been through a long dry spell of dating, would you take a chance? I've never been on a blind date or written a blog, but I need feedback. Besides, I've turned thirty; I need to mix things up a little in my life. You're invited along for the ride. Fasten your seatbelt; I think you'll need it.

I'm going to introduce myself with an alias. Yes, the names will be changed to protect the innocent, including me. Especially me. I'm calling myself Annika after the character in the Pippi Longstocking books. I loved how they were always eating cakes and drinking coffee. This love of sweets may have contributed to my slightly plump self. So call me Annika. My favorite store is Nordstrom so Annika Nordstrom is my nom de plume.

When the blind date idea was first suggested to me, I said "no way." I have a large family of mostly married siblings who recently decided that I've passed the legal limit for not dating in X-many years. I'm the first to admit I've had a dry spell. A lot of women would head over to

Match.com or some other online dating site, but I don't trust computers enough to hand over my love life to them. What if someone hit the wrong button and matched me up with Jack the Ripper?

Also, I believe in God, and while I believe He could use a cold, impersonal computer to introduce me to someone special, I have faith that He can handle this without the help of technology. I prefer to meet someone on my own. Okay, that isn't exactly happening, I know. Filtering through someone I trust is the next best thing, but I wasn't convinced of this when it was first suggested.

A few days ago, I turned thirty. I know it's not the end of the world if you're not married before you hit the big three-o; it certainly wasn't to me, but it seemed to flick on a switch in the part of my oldest sister's brain where the matchmaking center is located. At my birthday party, Ruth oh so casually brought up dating while she was slicing my cake. (Chocolate, of course. I used to love vanilla, but I can't eat it anymore. That's a whole blog post by itself.)

"So, Annika, how long has it been since you've had a date? Trent doesn't count." Subtle, isn't she? And of course Trent doesn't count; he's a friend of mine.

My answer went roughly, "I um, well, um. I'm not sure."

"That's what I thought," Ruth said and smiled not unlike a snake might right before it strikes (minus the flicking tongue). "I've been thinking about fixing you up with someone Brad knows." Brad is my sister's husband. He's tall, dark, and thin with a beard that I'm convinced he grew to hide behind. Everyone turned to look at him, and I swear you could see him in slow motion break out in a sweat. He stammered something about a cousin or a friend of a cousin, or maybe it was the cousin of a friend. Anyway, I gathered this guy isn't any more successful than I am at meeting someone. Ruth started describing how she is trolling, selling me to this guy. She almost has him reeled in, from the sound of it, and I'm just starting to feel slightly dismayed that I'm such a hard sell, when my middle brother, John, chimed in.

"I know a great guy from work. He's into animals, a real sweetheart of a guy. You'd love him!"

I didn't realize John was even working actually, but I could see I was being roped into going out with the sweetheart, animal guy, too. Even my mom got into it, murmuring about some long lost son of a friend or something.

The only one who didn't say anything was Grace, my younger sister. She just sat there smiling and eating cake. (I think she was on her second piece. She's petite and graceful. She can eat whatever she wants and never gain a pound. Obviously, I hate that.) She was enjoying this. No one was singling her out.

She should have had my back, right? Not only is she my roommate (we share a small, rented bungalow), but as the only other unmarried sibling, you'd think she'd want to stick together. I mentioned that to her at the time.

"Uh , Grace, a little help here. Keep in mind you're next in line to be married off."

"Annika never dates," she said, still smiling. You'll get yours someday, Grace. "And Annika loves dogs. Sounds like a perfect match with the animal guy."

"Does he have a brother for Grace?"

"Don't start on me; I'm nowhere near your age, Annika."

"Two years! I've got two years on you!"

"Anyway, everyone met and married their spouses in birth order."

Birth order? Really? That's the best she can do? "What is this, some medieval serfdom? Don't any of you people believe in God? Couldn't He toss someone across my path?"

Mom patted my hand. "Of course we do. But until that happens, you need a little help, dear."

Then Grace said, "You've barely dated since college."

"You can stop helping now, Grace."

Mom brought up my friend, Trent, then. "He's such a nice boy, Annika. Why haven't you ever been interested in him?" Sure, Mom, why don't I just date my brother? It'd be practically the same thing.

Then Ruth said it. "We do this because we love you, Annika." Yes, she played it that way, like they were staging an intervention. By the end of the evening, she had accused me of sitting on the sidelines of life and was insisting on setting up a date for me for next week with Brad's friend or cousin or whatever he is.

Well, I set my family straight. I can find a man on my own. I went to bed a little depressed. And not because it was a milestone birthday. I know I'm not a huge dater, but what was up with my family treating me like I desperately needed help finding a guy?

You feel for me, don't you? I would say it was the height of embarrassment, but I have a feeling a lot more is in store for me. I assume most of you will be women, so you can empathize with what I'm going through. What do you think? Feel free to leave comments and unload on my weird family. I have a birthday cake with my name on it.

* * *

I don't know if it was the pizza or the cake, but something gave me a nightmare. So now it's the middle of the night, and I can't sleep. I dreamed about Miss Martha, and it woke me up completely.

I hadn't even thought about Miss Martha in years. She was the old woman who lived down the street from us when I was in grade school. She was the kind to wear white cotton gloves and a small pillbox hat with netting over her face every time she went out, even if it was just to the laundromat on the corner or the grocery store.

We took turns helping Miss Martha carry her groceries up the stairs to her tiny, second-story apartment. We would always climb the rickety, narrow stairway very slowly behind Miss Martha as she pulled herself up step by step using both the railing and leaning heavily on her cane. I wish I could say we just liked to help out little old ladies, but she had a nicely-stocked candy dish that she invited us to sample to show her thanks when we finally arrived inside her apartment. Even though there was a bottom door that was locked, she locked the top one, too. So we had to wait on the skinny stairs while she fished her keys out of her giant, shiny black purse that hung on her elbow. I used to wonder if one day it would topple her.

Once inside, we waited by the door so we didn't track anything in on her pristine floor. She would insist on shakily pressing a quarter into our hands. Even though the place looked clean, in the spring her apartment reeked of mothballs, and it smelled just plain stale the rest of the time. White lace doilies that she had tatted were on every surface.

I hate to say it but she was a little on the stale side herself. The only conversation she would make was to ask us what we learned in school that day. She asked the question all year round, Saturday and Sunday included. I think she'd been a schoolteacher.

Well, in the dream it was the same as it was in my childhood. We climbed the steep stairs, but when the door opened, and the old maid with the pillbox hat pulled the netting from her face, instead of it being poor Miss Martha, it was me! I turned and said "What did you learn in school today, deary?" Then I fell down the stairs, overloaded purse, cane, and all.

I must have fallen out of bed, because I woke up on the floor, my heart racing.

I'll tell you the truth; earlier that evening I had no intention of going out with anyone that my family set me up with, but after that dream, they can't get in line fast enough. I sent a mass text to everyone in my family right then at three a.m. that I was willing to go on a blind date or two.

I'm going to fix myself a cup of hot chocolate and try to go back to sleep. Maybe I'll watch a little TV. Anything to get that image out of my head.

* * *

I'll bring you up to speed to save you reading all of the comments from my posts. The overwhelming majority of you agree with my family... and you don't even know me! I'm kind of surprised how many of you found me already. I guess the search engine must have brought my blog up for you, since this is anonymous.

Several suggestions ranged from taking supplements to meditation to avoiding sweets and losing a little weight. (You know who you are.) I kind of expected a little sympathy, but most of you commented that it sounded like fun to date a whole bunch of guys you'd never met before. I'll pass along my leftovers to you when I'm done if you live in my area.

That was a joke! You won't know where I live, part of the anonymity that is so important here if I'm going to bare my soul to you.

I've prayed about it, slept on it, mulled it over coffee and a cinnamon roll (one of those giant, luscious ones with the cream cheese frosting), and yes, I'm definitely doing it. What have I got to lose? A bunch of evenings, sure, some embarrassment, probably, but I'm ready for an adventure. Now before you say, "What are you thinking, dear Annika?" remember that I'm thirty, and I don't meet a whole lot of guys working as an accountant at a non-profit. It's time to let down my hair a little. Yes, it's only shoulder-length, and I'm a little uptight, but all the more reason to take this plunge. And don't forget Miss Martha. I haven't.

So I woke up on the couch this morning. I have a perfectly respectable bed, but I couldn't sleep after that frightening picture of my life. Also I was tossing and turning and trying to decide if this was adventurous or insane. There's a fine line, you know. The traitor, Grace, was leaning over me, shaking me awake.

When I sat up, my stiff neck didn't help the general anxiety that enveloped me. I had dreamed something after the Miss Martha nightmare; after I landed on the couch. I told Grace about my second dream, but not about the first. That was too embarrassing. The second one wasn't exactly a nightmare, just a vague uneasiness as I wandered everywhere looking for something.

Grace did not exude sympathy. "Car keys?" she suggested. "Are they hanging out with mine?" She followed that up with a suggestion to hurry, because she'd just discovered me on the couch. It was really late. She thought I was in my room getting ready.

Unfortunately, today was not the day to show up late. My new boss, Jack Grayson was giving a presentation this morning.

Grace asked if he was cute, which was typical. Then she went off on a hunt for her car keys. She was going to be late, too. Also typical.

Grace told me to wear something nice, because he could be Mr. Right. Hello, she sees me dress up every day for work! I always look nice. I haven't even met Jack yet, anyway.

I quickly surveyed myself in the full-length mirror on my closet door. I looked professional, but she wanted me to wear something extra special, like I had time for that after oversleeping. I shrugged. Jack Grayson better not be Mr. Right, because he would not be wowed by what was staring back at me. I hurried through my make-up and gathered my unruly, supersonic curly hair into a claw.

Tonight is my first date. It's with the sweetheart of a guy who loves animals. He works with my brother John. I thought John was working as a deejay at a radio station, but Grace said he works in road construction for the city or the county... or was it the state?

This is going to have to be a short post. I'm dictating it while I'm driving. Not that you should do that. Remember: cell phones down in the car. I'll throw that little public service announcement in for free.

Chapter Two

You would not believe the day I had. Let me start by saying I did not go on a blind date, so all of you who are reading just for the description of that can skip this post. If you'd like to hear how messed up a day can be, then keep reading.

Well, you might remember my last post had me oversleeping. The only thing available in the house for a quick breakfast was cold pizza, and I was not in the mood for coagulated grease. On the way to work, I spotted a new bagel place I've been meaning to try, and pulled into the drive-thru for a bagel and coffee. As I rolled down my window, I was hit with the unappetizing smell of burnt toast and skunk!

Now I don't want anybody writing to tell me how coffee smells like skunk. It does not! Don't be hating the brew! Remember, coffee is our friend.

Well, after the drive-thru skunk smell, I kept right on driving. Better to be hungry than to heave. Yes, I did just say that, but don't quote me.

So, even though I hurried, I was still late. When I arrived at work everyone was already in the conference room. I would have just gone right in, but my stomach was growling. Rather than have my noisy stomach interfere with the meeting, I went to the break room in search of a snack. Fortunately, some blessed soul brought in doughnuts. I snagged one and a cup of joe and tried to sneak into the meeting. Well guess where the only empty chair was? Right in front of the speaker, so I'm sure all eyes were on me. I would have apologized, but I've found in the past that is even more distracting.

Speaking of distracting, as soon as Jack saw me, he lost his place in his presentation. I also noticed a fairly puzzled look on his face. I wish I could say that my looks are so striking that men are enraptured when they see me, but I decided it was probably that I had powdered sugar on my face from the doughnut. I wiped my mouth with the back of my hand, and sure enough, there was the evidence. So I was thinking, what kind of man is that put off by a little sugar? I mean really.

Just to show what a big person I am, I went up to him after the meeting since he didn't introduce himself to me. I told him I was looking forward to having him join our team. He mumbled something and excused himself quickly. So I decided the guy is just weird. Good-looking, but most definitely weird. Maybe I shouldn't be saying that on a public blog, in case someone figures out who he is, but you know you were already thinking it.

I ran into Nadine right after that. She's the public relations person and a friend of mine. "The new boss was a little distant when he met me. I guess coming in late must have upset him. I overslept, though, and --"

Nadine almost choked on her coffee when she looked up at that moment. "What are you doing?" Nadine is kind of flamboyant, but wasn't she overdoing the whole you've-got-sugar-on-your-face thing? I was wondering when did everyone get so fastidious?

I was quickly power-walked to the bathroom where Nadine pointed out to me that I'd applied liner to only one eye, giving me a decidedly lopsided appearance. Well, that's what happens when you get in a hurry; you forget your eyeliner.   Oversleeping was making this day into a train wreck.

Do you suppose I brought my makeup bag to work on the one day of all days that I would need it? Of course not, and Nadine didn't have any eye liner either. She offered a black sharpie. That's what I get in the midst of my crisis, makeup humor.

I supposed I'd better stop and point out that was only a joke. Otherwise someone will use a sharpie on their eyes and I'll be sued. I'm not sure what for, but America loves to sue.

Nadine did have some lotion I could use to remove it. I had to take off the make-up from both of my eyes because otherwise I'd still look lopsided with the mascara on.

Well, you can guess what I looked like with no eye make-up; my eyes just disappear. I looked tired. So first I looked lopsided; then I looked tired. There is no way my boss is going to take a second glance at me. Or in this case, a third glance. That's what it will take before I finally get my makeup right, and it will be some other day.

Now Nadine is a true friend. She stayed right there with me while I wadded up toilet paper and removed every trace of eye makeup. So what does she do but bring up my last faux pas. "This is worse than when you wore one black shoe and one blue shoe to the Christmas party."

"That could have happened to anyone." In fact, I'll bet it's happened to one of you readers.

Of course, as Nadine pointed out, it could only happen to someone who buys the exact same shoe in different colors. I don't do that anymore, by the way.

Just as I was contemplating what office supplies I could use to substitute for foundation and blush, Nadine's lotion started making me itch.

"This lotion sure is itchy." In fact, it was making my eyes swell and my face break out in a rash. That's when I had a sudden, terrible thought. "This doesn't have aloe in it, does it?" I searched the tiny print for the ingredient list. I saw those terrible words right when Nadine said, "sure" nonchalantly like she hadn't just sealed my fate for three miserable days. I'm allergic to aloe.

Now before you all send me your home remedies, let me tell you that the only thing that works is Benadryl, and that makes me conk out.

Well, as I was frantically pumping soap out of the dispenser and washing off the lotion, Nadine was commenting on how fast the rash was covering my eyes and the surrounding area and how bad it looked. Everyone needs someone in her life to tell her what she doesn't want to hear, don't you know? Hardly helpful, Nadine.

So I know you're thinking "Annika, these things happen. Head for home and start slugging Benadryl. You'll be back to normal in a few days. " I would have loved to take a three-day nap; who wouldn't? But just then, Zoe, the receptionist, came into the restroom looking for me.

"Jack needs to go over the books with you, Annika. Oh!" This last exclamation upon seeing my face. "He's going to present to the board immediately afterward." She looked at Nadine who just shrugged. Zoe turned around and left without saying a word about my rash.

I decided on a half dose of medicine because a full would make me comatose and went to the break room to ice my eyeballs. After taking the medication, I couldn't put it off any longer; I knew I'd have to hurry before the Benadryl made me so drowsy I couldn't think. Jack's door was open, so I knocked and stood in the open doorway. A startled look came over his face when he saw me.

"I'm having an allergic reaction," I said to reassure him that I wasn't turning into Ms. Hyde before his very eyes. "We should probably hurry and go over the books before I start nodding off from the medication I had to take." I didn't bother to detail my makeup woes. He's got enough on his mind without having eyeliner explained to him.

Jack was quick to agree that we could finish up in no time. Anything to get the lunatic out of his office, I'm sure.

I could barely keep my eyes open by the time I finished explaining everything. I went to my office, closed the door, and put my head down on my desk.

* * *

No, I didn't go to sleep. Well, not exactly. I might have, but Nadine came in with a cup of coffee immediately and woke me; I mean, um, roused me.

Now I love coffee as much as the next person and probably more, but it needs cream. This was strong, and it was black. I could barely choke it down, but I did. It was really, just too hard to pull myself out of my desk chair and too far to stumble to the break room to get the powdered creamer that I hate anyway.

The plan was lots of coffee, half doses of meds, and keep all sharp objects and phones away from me. The way it worked out was I stared off into space a lot and dozed on my lunch hour, waking up with the imprint of the blotter on my face, like anyone would notice that with the rash. Grace couldn't pick me up until the end of the day. It was too much of an effort to call anyone else. No way I was taking the wheel of a car. Do policemen ticket zombies?

When I texted Grace, I saw a message from John telling me "Will" would pick me up at 6:00. I would have groaned aloud when I saw that message, except Zoe was standing there, and she already had been whispering on her phone all day; I assume about me. I hope in her gossip I come out as being medicated, not drunk or on drugs. One never knows with Zoe. She's the fastest gossip in the Midwest, but she doesn't always get things right.

Naturally, I tried to call John, but he didn't pick up his phone, as usual. I don't know why he even has a phone. It's either not charged, in his car, or on silent. I'm in the middle of an emergency, here, John... pick up! I can't even call his place of work and leave a message to have him call me. I couldn't remember if he worked for the county or was it the state? Yeah, not too happy to see that he gave Will my address. This is all new to me. Better to meet the guy at a restaurant. Might have been nice to get some details about Will other than his first name. Obviously, I was going to have to cancel with this guy to his face. Not looking forward to that.

We stopped at the pharmacy on the way home to buy up all their Benadryl, so I wasn't surprised there was a blue truck parked in front of the house when we drove up. I was a little surprised to see there were two people in the cab of the truck.

Grace was puzzled of course. "He brought a date on your date?"

As we got closer, we could see the second "person" was a big, black lab.

"A dog! He brought a dog on your date! Can John pick them or what?"

Grace parked the car and went in the house, stifling a laugh. As I approached the truck, the lab started barking.

"Quiet Coal!" I heard a command come from the cab. Coal did not stop barking.

Out of the truck stepped Will. Okay, he's cute in a cowboy sort of way. He looked like he worked out. He took off his Stetson and held out his hand for me to shake.

I had to raise my voice to be heard over the barking. "I'm sorry, Will. I'm having a little problem with an allergy, so I'm going to have to postpone our date for this evening."

Coal stuck his nose through the cracked window and sniffed. Then he returned to barking.

Will looked puzzled. "An allergy? Like hay fever?"

I pointed to the rash still very much in evidence. "No it's this rash on my face."

Now what he said next could either be considered kind of sweet or just odd. He said, "I can see how you might not want to go out in public looking like that. We could sit in a dark corner of the restaurant. I could loan you some sunglasses."

"Well, not only does it look awful, but it itches, so I have to take medicine that makes me drowsy," I said.

He nodded; then suddenly he looked horrified. "You aren't allergic to dogs, are you?"

I assured him the allergy was to aloe vera.

Cowboy Will looked immeasurably relieved. "Oh, okay, good. Do you think you'll be better by tomorrow?"

"Well it usually takes a few days, so it probably won't be cleared

23

up before Friday."

"Friday it is. Same time?"

I told him that was fine and offered to meet him at the restaurant, but he declined. I said goodbye and headed into the house.

Grace was peeking through a slat in the blinds. "Are you still going out?"

"Of course not, I'm taking a full dose of medicine and going to bed."

"Then why is he still out there?"

I looked and he hadn't moved at all. Grace checked periodically, and he was still there for quite a while. Finally I couldn't take it anymore. I went out to the truck. Both man and dog were sound asleep in the cab. Coal woke first and started barking. I had a weird deja vu feeling as Will got out of the truck and removed his hat. Would he introduce himself all over again?

"Is everything all right, Will?" I asked.

"Yes, ma'am, I guess I fell asleep."

"Okay, well... see you Friday." I went back inside.

"He said he fell asleep," I told Grace.

She peeked out the window. "Still there. Are you sure you want to go out with him. Is country even your type?"

"I don't think I have a type," I said.

"He's gone," Grace said.

Just then there was a knock at the door. Grace raised her eyebrows. "I could be wrong. Is this guy ever leaving?"

"It's getting a little creepy," I agreed.

Grace looked out through the peephole. "It's Trent," she said and opened the door.

Trent is my polar opposite in pretty much every respect. He's tall; I'm short. He's thin; I'm... not. The exception being we both love Asian food and can't get enough of it. We go out for Chinese several times a month just to keep caught up on what's going on in each other's lives. (And because of the aforementioned addiction. If I don't get crab Rangoon and egg rolls with hot mustard regularly, well, you don't want to know what will happen.)

When Trent started dating his girlfriend, Brooke, the three of us went out for Chinese to get to know each other. Um, we haven't been out since. It's not because I don't like her; she doesn't love Chinese like we do. I can take her or leave her. She's a single mom with a son. I forgot his name. Trent is an elementary school teacher. Her son is in Trent's class. Seems like a conflict of interest to me, but well, nobody asked me.

She's pretty with natural red hair, thin, elegant. How does she manage to pull off the elegant look when she has a child? She's this amazing artist, also. Right now she works the cosmetic counter at Macy's. I'm sure she's just perfect at that, too. She said she sees every woman's face as a blank canvas, or something like that. Do I need to say more?

Trent goes on and on about how great her paintings are. He's trying to help get her art noticed, or as he puts it "realize her potential." He's always helping her with her son, too. I think the kid's on the softball team Trent coaches.

Anyway, when he saw me, Trent squinted and said, "It's barely noticeable, Annika."

"That's how it works, Trent. If you squeeze your eyes shut, rashes and oh pretty much everything disappear."

"What?" he said shaking his head like he didn't know what I was talking about. I laughed.

I poured out to Trent the whole weird story. Then I told him about the blind date experiment I was about to begin.

"Cool," he said. That's about the response I'd expect from him. We're just friends after all. "I'll pray that God sends your way just the guy for you."

I met Trent my senior year of college while I was interning at an accounting firm. He came in to get his taxes done. His record-keeping was pathetic. He hadn't submitted a return the last year or two. He was still in college, but he had worked numerous jobs. He hadn't even collected all of his w-2s. When he found out how much it was going to cost to have his taxes done, he suggested swapping it for detailing my car. If he'd seen it, he wouldn't have bothered offering. The dirt was probably what was holding it together, that and some strategically placed duct tape. I had some windows that wouldn't roll down, though, so I told him if he'd fix them I'd cut him a deal. He got online and figured out how to do it from a video. Of course, I still had to pay the firm, but it was cheaper than taking my car to the auto glass place.

He asked me out once, probably just to be nice. It's obvious we're not attracted to each other. I told him I wanted to focus on school and my career.

He's the kind of friend you can turn to when you need help, because you don't want to call a family member who will never let you live it down. As the youngest members of the family, Grace and I have to put up with condescending tones and knowing looks passed between family members. I often feel like my siblings want to pat Grace and me on the head. "There, there, you'll grow up eventually." Trent has saved us several times from that fate. I'd tell you about them, but someday, someone might figure out who I am from my blog. then I'd have to hunt each one of you down and kill you.

Just kidding! Don't write me and tell me how gruesome that is. Can't you take a joke?

Some of you have mentioned you think I should be able to figure out a way to meet guys on my own. I'm sure that you all have tons of interesting ways to meet people, but I obviously do not. At my job, as financial officer of a nonprofit most of my contacts are numbers and spreadsheets. I'm going out with Will on Friday. You can't date a spreadsheet.

Chapter Three

I woke up the next morning itchy and rashy, looking like I'd rubbed my face in poison ivy. I stayed home from work.

Fast forward to Thursday. I feel better. I look better. A little strategic makeup and you'd barely notice the rash if you didn't stare. And you shouldn't stare anyway. It's rude.

So when I arrived at work the next morning, I picked up my messages from Zoe and stopped in Nadine's office. I'd barely said "hello" when our boss, Jack, stuck his head in.

"Good morning, Nadine. And Annika... how are you feeling?" He was impeccably dressed. He stepped all the way into the office and put his hand on my arm. He must be one of those touchy feely guys. Warm brown eyes like Lindor chocolate truffles looked into mine. The dark chocolate ones. I blinked, reminded myself he was my boss, and told him I was fine.

"Glad to have you back," he said. He patted my arm, smiled, and continued on to his office.

Nadine asked me about my birthday, and as I unloaded about the clan trying to marry me off, she spouted, "What is this, the dark ages? Are we returning to the days of arranged marriage?"

She grew pensive, studied me. "Now that you mention it, though, I do know someone, too. His name is Geoffrey. I've always thought you'd hit it off, but I didn't want to say anything because I didn't want to insinuate you couldn't get a date, but now that I know you're on the hunt for a guy..."

See how I'm surrounded by less than subtle people?

She lowered her voice, "Or for that matter, how about our new boss?"

I was startled. How did she know what I was thinking? "Jack?"

"Why not? He's good-looking, well-dressed, good manners. Or don't you find him attractive?"

"Well, first, whoever I date has to be a Christian." I was firm on that one.

"I figured as much. I think I saw a Bible on his desk once."

That was encouraging. He wasn't afraid to put his faith out there.

"Even if I were willing to date someone I work with, what do you want me to do, ask him out?" I laughed.

Nadine didn't join me. "Women do ask men out now, you know."

Obviously she doesn't know me as well as she thinks she does. "Not this woman."

"So, you'll let people set you up with someone you've never met, but if you know him, he's off limits unless he makes the first move?"

I thought it over for a few seconds. "That pretty much sums it up."

"Okay, if you won't ask him, how about you just make him aware that you're willing to go out?"

"How do I do that?"

"I think we've just discovered why you don't date."

"I date!"

"When?"

"Well, I couldn't come up with a specific day and month off the top of my head," I bluffed.

She called me on it. "A year?"

I didn't say anything. In my defense, I've been concentrating on my career.

"You know this stuff naturally, Annika. You've just stifled it." Does she realize how insulting that sounds?

"Stifled it? Just because I don't throw myself at men doesn't mean there's something wrong with me."

"There isn't anything wrong with you; you just don't flirt."

"I flirt!" Why was I getting defensive about this?

"I've never seen you flirt."

"We've always worked in an all-girl office. Actual men have to be present for flirting to take place."

"Well, now we have Jack. You have to act like you like him, but in a very subtle way, so he thinks it's his idea." She took out a good-sized mirror and puffed up her hair.

"How do I do that?"

"Well, I can't follow you around at work and give pointers. But take for instance just now when Jack came in. What did you do?"

"I said 'good morning' and smiled."

"You said 'good morning' and let him pass you by. You have to engage him."

"Engage him?" That sounded weird.

"Yes, I just started reading about it in a book called 'Rules of Engagement.' You have to make him look at you, have a conversation with you. Engage him." She pulled a book out of her drawer. Does she think I need to read a whole book on dating? I looked at the back cover. It was written by a husband and wife team. They were both gorgeous. I handed it back to Nadine.

"Well, I'll engage the next guy. I don't think I ought to flirt with my boss." Nadine's phone rang right then.

She picked it up and whispered, "Maybe not. You do want to keep your job, after all."

I left thinking maybe we should have lowered our voices earlier.

There wasn't anyone close by that I saw, but I didn't want everyone thinking I am inept at dating.

As I walked by Jack's office, I slowed down. I could see him adjusting his tie in front of a mirror in a closet and checking his teeth for food. I felt kind of bad for spying on him, although let's be honest; he wasn't exactly hiding his primping. He turned from the mirror. I hurried on to my office, closed the door, and leaned on it.

I whispered to myself "Engage him. You have to engage him." I think I need practice before my blind date tomorrow, and Jack was friendly, maybe even interested. Perhaps a lot of men had been interested and were just waiting for a signal from me, waiting for me to engage them. Definitely something to think about... later. I'd love to sit around blogging with all of you faithful followers, but I have two days' worth of work to do.

By the way, someone commented that I should date Trent. You need to go back and read the first blog post. He's like a brother to me. Besides, he's dating someone else.

* * *

Crazycatlady has commented that my boss, Jack, seems all wrong for me. I barely know the guy, and you hardly know me. Let's stick to facts, people.

Near the end of the day I ran into Nadine when I went to get some supplies. She pulled me into her office and shut the door. Turns out she thinks I need practice, too, before my blind date, so she wants to go out after work.

"So I can practice engaging men?"

"Yes!" She seemed to be enjoying this way too much. I was instantly suspicious.

"Why are you so excited?"

She had a big smile on her face. "I just think it will be fun; that's all."

"Fun? Or funny?"

"It might be an amusing way to spend a Thursday evening..."

"... watching me make a fool out of myself!"

"Not necessarily."

"So where do I find these men who are dying to meet me?"

"Who said they were dying to meet you? You have to make them want to meet you."

"By engaging them."

"Exactly."

"Where does all of this engaging take place?"

"I have a place in mind."

"I'm not going to a bar," I said firmly.

"I figured as much. I'm way ahead of you, and it's not a bar."

"Well, I hope this place has food. I'm already starving. What time is it anyway?"

"It's almost quitting time, but food will have to wait. Grab your stuff. I'll drive."

Food will have to wait? We live in America. Food is everywhere all the time. Why does she think they invented the drive-thru? It was specifically so people like me who are starving to death don't have to miss a meal. Or wait for a meal. Or have hunger pangs. Or set one foot out of their vehicle to do so.

On the way to the car, I can see she's looking me over. "Annika, you've got to think of yourself as a product you're selling."

Well, I can tell you I set her straight on that point. I am not for sale.

"That's not what I mean. Think of how you present yourself as a marketing campaign. When a new product is for sale, what do you think is one of the first things that is considered? Packaging. En voila!"

She swept her hand in a vertical gesture to herself. Nadine always looks very put together. Studying her, I realized it was her accessories that made her stand out.

"The name is very important." She said my real name and called it odd. I've gotten that my whole life. "What's your middle name?"

"Marie."

"Nope, that won't work. Your first name does sound foreign."

"It's Swedish."

She brightened. "Can you fake a Swedish accent?"

"For the rest of my life? I'm hoping to get married some day."

"Forget the name." She drove to a nearby spot and parked.

I looked around. "This is a gym."

"Welcome to the twenty-first century. They're called fitness centers, now."

I wrinkled up my nose. "I'm not into sweating or the smell of anyone else sweating or muscle-bound men. I was hoping he'd be more interested in me than in how pumped up he is."

"Every guy in here won't look like the Incredible Hulk. You want someone who's fit, don't you?"

"I hadn't thought about it."

"Trust me, you do."

"Couldn't I learn to engage men at a restaurant or the grocery store? I haven't eaten in forever." I looked through my purse for a stick of gum.

"We're doing a different kind of shopping, a little window shopping. And for future reference, most guys don't go out to eat alone. They go through the drive-thru. And single men don't go to the grocery store until late Sunday night when they suddenly realize they're completely out of food for the week. The rest of the time all of those juicy men you see are just picking up food for the wife and kiddies."

What makes a man juicy? Will had looked pretty strong. Would Nadine consider him juicy?

She was already on her way in, so I ran to catch up. I could be a good sport about this, no pun intended. After all, in her own weird way, Nadine was just trying to help. When we reached the entrance, Nadine stopped with her back to the door, blocking it, studying me. I was wearing black pinstriped pants and a pale blue silk blouse. I thought I looked pretty good.

"Unbutton your blouse."

"What?"

"Just a button or two."

"What have you got in mind for me here? And just what kind of book is this 'Rules of Engagement'? I'm not out to seduce men."

Nadine sighed. "I'm not having you seduce men. You won't be showing any cleavage. You just look all stiff and formal, buttoned up the way you are. A fitness center is more relaxed than an office."

"Oh brother." I did it though.

"Untuck your blouse, too."

"Now I just look wrinkled."

"No, you're fine. Now we're going in here and tell them we're interested in joining and want to look around."

"So... lie."

"*I'm* interested. Then we walk around and ask the guys working out what they think of the facility. Now to engage them you have to say more than just 'Do you like the treadmills here?' You have to comment on how hard the lift they're doing looks. Things like that."

"Oh Mr. Weightlifter, you're so strong and manly," I said in my best ditzy voice.

"Annika, you're going to have to take this more seriously, if it's going to work. Be sophisticated."

I can do sophisticated. I switched to my low, sultry voice. "Oh, Mr. Weightlifter, you're so strong and manly."

"That's vampy."

"I want to suck your strong and manly blood," I said, still sultry,

38

but with a Transylvanian accent.

"I said 'vampy' not vampire-y, and that's disgusting, by the way." She sighed. I guess my sense of humor must be a great trial to her.

"Just watch me." She went inside and led the way to the unattended desk, which offered an inviting bowl of peppermints.

"Don't say anything," she warned over her shoulder. When she turned back around a man had appeared from the room behind. I grabbed a handful of mints.

"May I help you?" The man was very good looking, very strong, and yes, very manly. I was sure he must be considered juicy.

I whispered to Nadine, "This is a great idea!" and put on my best engaging smile as I unwrapped a mint.

She grabbed my arm, making me drop my mint, and pulled me back a few steps, positioning herself between me and Fitness Center Guy.

"Change of plans. I get this one," she whispered.

"Hey! I thought we were out shopping for a guy for me!"

Nadine glared at me. "Keep your voice down! Remember we're only window shopping. Besides, you've already got a date for tomorrow night." She turned and smiled at the guy behind the desk.

Holding out her hand for Fitness Center Guy to shake, she said, "I'm Nadine Lewis. This is Annika Nordstrom. I'm interested in joining and was hoping we could look around."

"I'm Tom Carter. I'd be happy to show you around." I noticed Nadine held on to Tom's hand a little longer than necessary. Is that part of engaging? For the next hour, he gave us a tour, showing us every amenity the place offered. I think they both forgot I was there. I didn't get to engage any of the hunky guys we passed.

When we reached the front again, Tom gathered up a bunch of brochures and gave them to Nadine. They exchanged business cards, too.

"That was a complete waste of time," I said on the way to the car.

Nadine pointed her key at me. "That was not a waste of time at all. You got to observe me engaging Tom." She smiled and looked at his business card.

"Right, I was taking notes the whole time. Very educational."

Nadine nodded. "I thought so."

"I was being sarcastic!" We got in the car and drove the few blocks back to work. Nadine parked next to my car.

"What I learned is that 'engaging' is not for me. If a guy can't tell I'm interested without me pursuing him, then he isn't interested enough in me."

"You can go that route, but it will weed out a lot of possibilities in the man department."

"Hopefully, it will help me weed out the rotten tomatoes." I gathered up my things to get out of the car.

"I suppose you think that God will bring Mr. Right to you."

"If God isn't involved in this part of my life, then He isn't involved in any of it. I can trust him." Of that I am sure.

"So you're going to continue hiding in your accounting office. Continue not taking chances?"

"I'm willing to go on some blind dates. After all, I don't have a lot of opportunities to meet many men. And I'm not hiding!"

"But you'll do it without the 'Rules of Engagement' method."

"I'll do it without any method. It'll just be me. See you tomorrow, Nadine."

After I got home, I told Grace about what happened. Turns out she'd had a few college classes with Tom. Neither of us thought he was right for Nadine or me.

Another thing... Would Nadine have tagged along after me the way I just had after her? Even though we're about the same age, Nadine doesn't seem in any hurry to get married. I think she sees dating as a way of life.

I'm willing to go on a few blind dates until I meet Mr. Right, but it occurs to me that I might have to go on some bad ones too. Tomorrow it all begins. Wish me luck!

Chapter Four

Mommyninjawarriorprincess suggested Grace chaperone these dates. I think since these are being set up by mostly family members that I shouldn't need a chaperone. The commenter also suggested I not listen to Nadine about the flirting. Read closer people. I'm obviously not taking Nadine's advice.

Aren't you just dying to know what happened on my first ever blind date? Well, in case you've already guessed, Will brought his dog again. He was already parked in front of the house when I pulled into my driveway. He's prompt; I'll give him that.

He got out and stood hat in hand, yelling at his dog as I approached his truck. He was dressed in jeans and another plaid western-type shirt, so obviously this was going to be a casual date. Good to know how to dress. I told him I'd just be a minute and hurried into the house.

Grace was spying again. She turned from the window when I came in. "Where can he possibly be taking you that he can bring his dog?"

I had no idea.

"What are you going to wear?"

"He's wearing jeans, so I will, too."

Grace told me she thought I was a good sport, and how it was a great idea to go out on a casual date and get to know one another without trying to impress each other. "Get to know the real Will" as she put it. I think she was trying to make me feel better, but honestly, I didn't care what we wore.

In the back of my mind, though, was the niggling thought "What if my brother John had talked him into this?" What if Will didn't really want to do it? He didn't seem to be putting forth much effort. He brought his dog; what's up with that?

I changed into jeans and a bright blue sweater, dashed on some perfume, refreshed my make-up, and said a quick prayer on the way out that amounted basically to "Thy will be done."

I grabbed my purse off the table near the door. Feeling like I forgot something, I looked around.

"Do you have your cell phone and your keys?" Grace said.

"Yes, mother, and I have some mad money, too. Don't wait up."

Grace stayed in the doorway watching me walk to the car. She called out, "Text me where you're going!"

I waved in a noncommittal way. I had no plans to spend my date texting my little sister.

Will put a leash on Coal and let him out of the truck to "get to know me" which amounted to the dog sniffing every inch of me he could

44

reach. Then Will let him get up in the truck and got in himself. It was

obvious he was not opening the door for me. Strike one. I got into his very

tall truck with some difficulty and no help. The dog plopped down.

"He likes you." Will sounded very confident.

"How can you tell?"

"He didn't growl at you."

Did I just pass some weird initiation? If the dog hadn't liked me,

would the date have ended right then? What if Coal changed his mind? I

inched farther away from him, but the more I inched, the more the dog

sprawled. Eventually I was wedged up next to the door as Coal stretched

out between us.

We started off, and Will rolled both windows all the way down.

My hair started blowing all over the place.

"Um, Will, could we roll up the windows or turn on the air or

something? All of this wind is a little hard on my hair."

Will said, "I guess we could. Coal isn't used to perfume."

Coal isn't used to perfume? I know, you think he was kidding. I

can assure you that I learned by the end of the evening, Will doesn't kid.

He rolled up the windows a little. With my ultra-curly hair, I looked like

I'd ridden to the restaurant in a tornado by the time we arrived.

I was determined not to be put off by the dog. I ignored him as much as humanly possible. "What do you do, Will?"

He looked puzzled. "I work with your brother."

Oh yeah, oops. "So what do you do for the city?"

"County."

Oops again. Whatever. John changed jobs more often than some people change their sheets. I can't be expected to remember what he's doing all the time. Not to mention, I've got a lot of siblings.

"I do road construction."

"That must be hard work, especially when it was so hot this summer."

"Hard work is good for you. I'd go bonkers sitting behind a desk all day." He stopped at a traffic light and petted Coal. His tail thumped, hitting my purse. I moved it away from him. "What do you do?" he asked.

"I sit behind a desk all day," I laughed. He nodded. "I do the books for a non-profit."

He didn't comment on my job. We sat in silence for a few minutes. Okay.

"It's only temporary, though," he finally said.

"No, it's permanent. I've worked there for several years," I said.

"I mean my job. I'm going to have my own place some day, as soon as I save up enough money."

That was encouraging. He sounded responsible. "What kind of house are you saving up for?"

He shook his head. "The house doesn't matter. I'm going to have my own ranch."

Living in the Midwest, I can tell you there might be what was termed farming going on nearby, but not a whole lot of ranching. "Where would you ranch?"

"Out West, maybe Montana."

"Did you grow up there?"

"I'm from around here, but I spent summers on my uncle's ranch in Montana."

"That must have been fun."

"It's a great life."

We pulled in to Texas Roadhouse. Why was I not surprised? Will turned off the car and reached around behind the seat for something. He put Coal's leash on him and a blue vest with "Service Dog in Training" printed on it. He opened the door and led Coal out. I got out when it was obvious once more that he was not going to open the door for me.

"Coal is a service dog?"

"Nah, I got this vest from my cousin. She trains dogs for the blind."

"Isn't that lying?"

"What does it hurt? He'll behave himself. He's alone all day while I'm at work. I don't like to leave him alone all night, too."

Strike two. If a man will lie about something small and insignificant, will he tell the truth to me about bigger things? I'm not willing to take a chance. I probably should have left right then, but he kind of caught me off guard.

I'd never been to Texas Roadhouse before. It's loud. Very loud. The noise level seemed fitting for this night. Since we had to shout to be heard over the music, and Will obviously wasn't much of a talker anyway, we didn't attempt a whole lot of conversation.

Texas Roadhouse is very rustic in the decoration department beginning with a large water trough that held silverware wrapped up in napkins. At one point our server got up in a line with the rest of the servers and did a dance. That added a little flavor to the evening, never been anywhere where they did that before. The food was good, too. I had the fried chicken.

So it was a fun, though loud atmosphere, but after an evening of Will paying more attention to his dog than he did to me, I was ready to go as soon as I finished my chicken. Will was a slow eater, though, no doubt because he fed Coal bits of his steak all night.

At first Coal sat next to Will on the booth seat. We had dogs when I was growing up, but they didn't sit on a chair next to us at the table! When I saw the manager heading toward us, I excused myself to go to the restroom. When I returned, Coal was on the floor.

Will asked me if I was done with my fries. I said, "Knock yourself out." Not surprised that he fed them to Coal.

After we got in the truck, Coal decided to investigate something in my purse, maybe the leftover peppermints from the gym. Anyway, when I shoved his nose out of my purse and moved it to the other side of me, Will gave me a look.

"Don't like dogs, much, huh?"

How to answer? "I love dogs, but a girl's purse is sacred." "Not nosy ones!" or perhaps, "They're great on a bun with relish!"

I decided on the last one, just for a joke. I'd forgot that Will didn't have a sense of humor. He was not amused. Strike three. He obviously wasn't enjoying the date too much, because he drove me straight home. He opened the truck door for me this time, no doubt to get me moving faster. I thanked him for supper and headed inside.

So my date ended with a rather anti-climactic feel to it. I'll head off the question at the pass. Of course he didn't kiss me, but right before I got out of the truck, Coal did! So, no hard feelings, Coal.

* * *

Several of you agree with commenter Annikawhatareyouthinking who said I should have ended the date when Will pulled out the dog vest. No disagreement here. Someone is under the impression that I am a people-pleaser. There is a fine line between being polite and being a people-pleaser. I want to be a God-pleaser, and while that means sticking to my guns when something is outright wrong, please note that I did not lie and bring the dog in. That was all Will. My conscience is clear.

I have a friend who met the man who would be her husband on her first blind date. Obviously that did not happen with me, but life's an adventure, right? No more Spectator Annika sitting on the sidelines. On to Date Number Two. Or rather on to what I guess you would call a semi-date.

When I went in to work the next day, Nadine was dying to hear about Will. As I was describing what happened, Jack poked his head into Nadine's office. As we exchanged greetings Nadine was giving me "the look" that meant "do something and do it now!" I'd already told her I wasn't going to flirt with the boss, so I ignored her.

Jack brought up a financial report that needed clarification. I offered to explain it to him right away, but he glanced at his watch and told me he had what would amount to an all-day meeting on the other side of town with our consultant, and had just stopped in to get his briefcase that he'd forgotten. I let him know my schedule for the rest of the day. To my surprise he suggested lunch at Nunzio's (which just so happens to be one of my favorite Italian restaurants).

I'm sure you're thinking "Why is she calling this even a semi-date? It's a work meeting with her boss. She's pathetic." Well, maybe you won't think I'm so pathetic when you hear what happened.

After he left, Nadine closed her door and smiled, just stood there and smiled.

"What?" I asked.

She kept smiling.

"It's not a date," I insisted, "and I didn't ask him, either."

"No, it's not a date. It's a *lunch meeting*." I didn't like the way she said that.

"Right," I said, pulling open her door. After all, I have nothing to hide. "Lunch."

"No, it's what you're doing *after* lunch that matters," she said.

Zoe looked around. She sits right outside Nadine's office. I shut the door. "After lunch, I'm returning to work, and he's returning to his

51

meeting, Nadine."

She just smiled. Ever notice how something as simple as a smile can be so irritating?

I left.

I'll admit she made me nervous. This was just a lunch meeting, wasn't it? Nothing more? I went to my office and paced. Maybe he overheard us talking about Will. Maybe he read my blog? I know you're thinking that. I don't see how it could be that widespread yet, but even if he did, he wouldn't recognize himself. Remember I've changed the names.

Or would he?

I had an uneventful morning and headed for Nunzio's at the appointed time. Jack was already there at a table in the back. It was the darkest part of the restaurant. Even though it was daylight outside, inside it was all candles and mood lighting where we sat, with sconces that gave off a glow for their ambiance rather than for their lighting capability. I could barely see the menu.

I was a little nervous, but I don't think it showed, especially since it was so dark in there. Jack certainly seemed at ease.

I'd brought the financial report with me to go over with him. Jack was chatty and lighthearted, pulling out his cell to illuminate the report since the light was so dim. We laughed about that. It didn't take long; we had the working part of the lunch meeting over before our food came.

Jack was very funny and not smooth exactly, but something akin to it, charming perhaps. I don't necessarily like them smooth, but it works for him. He did pull his chair very close to mine while we were going over the report and didn't move it after we were done, so it would have looked to any innocent bystander like we were having an intimate lunch.

It looked that way to me, too.

I finally got a chance to explain to him what happened that first day with the missing eyeliner, and we had a good laugh over it. He did a lot of the touchy feely stuff, all in an appropriate way, of course.

After we finished lunch, I figured I'd just head back to the office, but Jack seemed in no hurry to leave. So we sat chatting for a long time. He insisted we have dessert, and when I said I couldn't possibly eat one of Nunzio's giant rich desserts, he insisted we split one. Don't say you expect me to turn down tiramisu, because we know that wasn't happening. Also, don't leave comments about germs and ruin it for me. Germs are so unromantic!

We didn't talk shop. Instead we talked about what we like to do, our families, what it was like growing up. We're both from large families. We have a lot in common. We both went to work at a non-profit when we could have made more money at a big corporation because we want to help people, and we both love chocolate!

On the way out, he held the door for me and walked me to my car. He was a perfect gentleman in every way. When I left, he put his hand on my hand that was resting on the car door, and said he'd see me tomorrow.

So you see why I called Date Number Two a semi-date. It wasn't exactly a full-fledged date, because we went over that report for a couple of minutes. But I think he just used that as an excuse to invite me out. I'm so excited to see where this will go!

* * *

So many Asian places, so little time. There are about fifty of them in our town. In the spirit of adventure, Trent and I have been on a mission to visit every restaurant. We'd decided we wouldn't frequent the same one twice until we've been to them all. We're saving the dives for last, hoping they'll go out of business. Obviously, I can't say the real names of these places in this blog because that would give away my location. We're about halfway through the list. I've kept track of what we thought of them. Maybe that will be my next blog when I'm done with this one. Assuming this blog experiment is successful, and I meet the man of my dreams.

Otherwise, I might abandon the whole blog experience. Of course I don't literally dream about men, except perhaps terrorists and others that chase me with knives or guns. Yeah, so not kidding about that one.

Trent and I met up at Asian restaurant #27 after work. He is usually cool about things, but this time he dived right into a delicate subject. He brought up my blind date experiment before we'd even ordered.

"So, Annika, what is the point of dating so many guys?"

"So many? Um, it's been like two, Trent."

"You're just at the beginning, though. There will be a lot of guys coming your way, Annika. Why? You've always been so gung ho in advancing your career. What happened to that?"

"I think I'm pretty settled in my career now, Trent."

"Are you lonely, Ann?" Obviously, he didn't call me Ann, but it was a shortened version of my name. He never does that. He knows I hate it. I didn't mention it to him because I was concentrating on the lonely part. Am I lonely? I have a large family I see often, a fulfilling job with good coworkers, and a roommate who's always there, for goodness sake. An honest question from a friend deserves an honest answer, but it was too awkward to admit. So I deflected it instead.

"How could I be lonely?"

I took a drink of water. Trent looked at me without saying anything. The waitress came just then and we ordered. After she walked away I brought up the weird decor of the place. Anything to keep from concentrating on me and my loneliness.

The place was done in Chinese modern with a plastic twist. I later decided if we'd gone through the drive-thru, we'd think everything was great and kept coming. The food tasted good, especially the appetizers, which of course are the most important part. I don't want to go back again, though, and it's the tree's fault.

We were seated by a plant. When I first sat down, I didn't even see the fake ficus behind us. It wasn't until I was served my Hunan chicken that I felt like I was being watched. That's when I noticed the ficus looking over my shoulder. Normally I don't mind a nosy plant, especially a fake one, since they don't eat much, but this one tapped me on the shoulder. I know you doubt me, but it happened! Maybe there is a logical explanation, like the air conditioning came on, causing the leaves to rustle. Or perhaps it was a cry for help.

Anyway, this plant had been abandoned, left to its own devices; I guess because it didn't need to be watered. There were several layers of dust upon dust... upon dust. I probably shouldn't have been worried. No way an ordinary feather duster could have budged a speck of that dust, so it wasn't going to fall on my food. A power washer might have taken care of it. Maybe. It made me wonder about the condition of the deep fryer where my crab Rangoon and egg rolls were prepared and the prep table where the house hot mustard sauce was mixed. It was good sauce, too. If you barely paint it on your egg roll and it still burns off a few taste buds, you know it's high quality stuff.

The next thing that happened may have you doubting my sanity if you don't already. I kept stealing glances at that plant. I actually felt a kinship to the ficus! We were both feeling a little pathetic just then, abandoned, relegated to be part of the forgotten decor. Maybe because we were both so self-sufficient. We required so little care. I had to excuse myself to visit the restroom.

I looked at myself in the chipped mirror and wondered if I was losing it if a plant could practically bring me to the verge of tears. What I saw looking back at me gave me hope. I'm normal, not pathetic, just a little preoccupied. I've spent a lot of years targeting my career. And maybe I was afraid, too. Afraid that I'd make a mistake when I picked... him. Afraid to fail at marriage. It was easier, after all, to concentrate on my job. Now it's time to focus on the next part of my life. Marriage and eventually a family.

There was a small fake sunflower sitting on a stand. I rinsed the dust off, returned it to its place, and headed back to the table. I didn't know about Trent, but I was ready to leave.

Fake plants and loneliness aside, I also got a lesson in getting food to go. Always visit the inside of a restaurant at least once to get a feel for its cleanliness. Don't just do takeout!

Chapter Five

Crazycatlady commented that she thought Jack was moving a little fast. If it felt that way in my blog post, then I must be miscommunicating. Really, it was all very appropriate.

You know that saying "when it rains, it pours"? Today I got drenched dating-wise. My mom called when I arrived home tonight. She's already set me up with someone! Kind of. I think it would be okay if I went out with him. One lunch with your boss does not a relationship make.

It's the son of my mother's friend, Karen. Mom has two good friends named Karen. One is pretty hip for her age, and the other is a dinosaur. I'm hoping it's the son of the fun one.

So, I'm being open-minded, of course, but listen to how this conversation with my mom went. First, she gave me his phone number.

"So, um, Mom, why am I calling Linus?" No, that's not his real name. Who would name their kid Linus?

"He's a little shy, Annika."

I can understand shy, so I gloss over that. "Is he my age?"

She was a little vague on that point. I figured she didn't know. Oh, she knew; believe me, even if she didn't know exactly, she definitely knew a ballpark figure. Whatever that means. When I think ballpark, I think of Wrigley Field and loaded Chicago dogs. This conversation was making me hungry.

"What's he like? Have you met him?"

It turns out she had met him, but she couldn't exactly place him. Does that sound as odd to you as it did to me?

Then I remembered she'd mentioned at my birthday party that a friend had a long lost son that was available. When I mentioned it, she hedged.

"Long lost son? I don't think I said that, Annika."

I know she said something like it. I just couldn't remember what.

"How could he be her long lost son? She didn't give him up for adoption. I need to go, Annika. You're father's waiting for me to go out to dinner."

Very unusual behavior for my mother. I weighed whether or not to call Linus. It goes against my rule of never asking a guy out, but if I didn't call, it might hurt his feelings, although how it could, I don't know because I've never met him. I stopped biting on my thumbnail and called.

I wasn't sure he answered at first. I figured we had a bad connection, so I said "hello" again loudly.

He said "hello."

I identified myself. He didn't say anything so I gave the long explanation. "I'm Annika Nordstrom. I'm the daughter of Vicky, your mother's friend."

I think he said "hi."

Okay, so was I supposed to suggest we go out? What was the protocol here? I was wishing I hadn't called.

I said I'd met his mother before, and that she was very nice. That was the truth; both Karens are nice.

He thanked me. I think.

He mumbled something about meeting my mother years ago. Okay. We both have mothers. I'm glad we got that out of the way. So I moved on to the next safest subject I knew: occupation.

I told him that I am an accountant for a non-profit and asked what he did. I couldn't hear the answer very well, but I think he said something like he works at a shelter. I said giving back to the community is very important. He agreed. I think. There was a long silence.

"Are you still there, Linus?" I said. "This connection is bad."

He was still on the line, so I said it would be fun to go out for dinner. When no suggestions came from the other end of the phone, I decided it might be best to keep it casual and suggested That Pizza Place. I didn't have any other plans for dinner and Grace was working late, so I suggested we meet tonight. After a few seconds I heard him agree. I suggested 6:30 and we got off the phone.

What a relief it was to hang up. You'd think in this age of technology that they could make cell phones that you can hear people on.

I didn't leave a lot of time to get ready and get over there. I'll write more when I get back.

* * *

I'm writing this from the restaurant. Now before you think I'm rude, listen to what has happened so far.

First, I was a couple of minutes late, but only a couple. When I arrived, I looked all over the restaurant. There was no guy sitting alone. So I told the hostess I was meeting someone here. She asked what he looked like and got a funny look on her face when I said I didn't know. Something like a mix of understanding and pity.

"I think he's already here. He's in the restroom."

She seated me. Fifteen minutes later, he still hadn't shown up, so I went over to her. "Are you sure he's in the restroom?"

"I'll send someone in to check for you," she said, not looking me in the eye.

I sat back down at my table. She came over almost immediately. "Yes, he's still in there." She turned to go, but I was beginning to get worried about him. I grabbed her arm.

"Is he okay?" I said.

She looked pained. There's no other word for it.

She said quietly, "Our cook said he's in there throwing up."

"Do you think it's food poisoning?" I said it as softly as I could. I hated to use that term in a restaurant. There was a couple seated next to us. The woman looked up from her menu at me.

"He didn't order any food yet. I'm sure he'll be fine." The hostess dropped her voice lower. "I think he's a little nervous."

Nervous? About a date with me? If I were a pizza, I'd be cheese. Well, maybe I'd be crazy bread, but either way, I'm totally benign.

He came out right then. He looked pale. It must be awful to be sick in a pizza restaurant. You can't get away from the smell. The hostess brought him over to my table. He slid into the booth, and kind of melted into the seat, like mozzarella on hot pepperoni. He looked not a day over eighteen.

I stuck out my hand. "I'm Annika Nordstrom. It's nice to meet you."

"Linus Peterson," he shook my hand limply.

I cannot tell you how much I wanted to pull out the hand sanitizer from my purse and apply liberally, but I restrained myself. I opened my menu and looked at the choices.

Our waitress came over then. I smiled at Linus over my menu. "What do you like on your pizza?"

Linus closed his eyes. "I don't think I could eat anything right now," he said quietly.

Should I have ended the date right then? I was weighing if I should suggest that, but the waitress was starting to look a little impatient, and I was hungry. I decided I'd order, and if he didn't feel better by the time the food came, I'd just get it to go. He wasn't volunteering what he liked. Pizza was turning out more complicated than I thought it would be. Then it occurred to me that since I invited him, I'd just order what I liked and pay for it myself. I closed the menu and handed it to her. "I'll take a large with everything on it."

Linus opened his eyes then and opened his menu. I could see his eyes running over the items until he must have come to what I ordered. He closed the menu. I rushed to put him at ease.

"My treat since I invited you. Especially since you don't feel well."

I could see this idea didn't set well with him. In fact, I think it upset him more that I suggested I pay.

"So what is that like working at a homeless shelter? It must be wrenching to see people in those circumstances," I said.

"I wouldn't know," he said quietly, "since I work at the animal shelter."

I would have been embarrassed if I simply hadn't been paying attention, but the guy mumbles. Even in person I could see that it wasn't the phone's fault that I couldn't hear him earlier. I could barely hear him now.

I apologized anyway. "Sorry. We must have had a bad connection when we talked earlier."

"I could hear you just fine," he said.

That's because I make it a point to speak clearly. Does he want me to tell him he mumbles? Because I was not planning on going there. This was supposed to be fun. I had a better time with my boss at lunch today. And he was my boss!

"Aren't phones funny that way?" I said. "That a connection could be bad on just one end?"

I'll never know how he felt about the fascinating subject of cell phone reception, because at that moment he excused himself and headed for the restroom. When the woman at the table next to us saw him go into the restroom again, she whispered something to the man with her, and they left.

I finally remembered how my mom described him that first night. She didn't call him Karen's long lost son. She called him Karen's invisible son. And he was proving to be just that.

So there we are. Here I sit waiting for him to return. I hope my pizza comes soon, because I am starving. I looked around, and since I didn't see him, I used my hand sanitizer. Just to be on the safe side, I'm going to eat with a knife and fork.

Chapter Six

Linus never did come out of the restroom. I mean, I'm sure he did at some point;   he didn't spend the night, but he must have slipped quietly away while I was eating. After I was done and had the rest of the pizza boxed up, I asked the waitress to have the cook check the restroom, and Linus was gone. I guess this must have been one of the most embarrassing nights of his life, but I don't know what else I could have done. I was trying to be friendly and put him at ease.

Someone commented that I should screen these dates better since I could end up dating someone who is underage! I said Linus looked eighteen. I'm sure he wasn't that young and definitely wasn't younger.

When I went home and told Grace about Date Number Three, she laughed. I'm glad that my love life can entertain her. It wasn't entertaining me too much. Two bad dates in a row! Well, two bad dates separated by a really good semi-date.

Speaking of Jack, when he came in the next day, he stopped at my office and told me how much he enjoyed our lunch. And when I came back from running an errand, a bag of Lindor chocolate truffles was on my desk. This candy is too good. I didn't ask where it came from, but I was pretty sure it was from Jack. After all, it matches his eyes.

I went in to see Nadine to tell her about our lunch meeting, but she was on the phone. I was kind of disappointed. I know I can tell her about it later, but I wanted to gloat a little that it went so well. The other night when we went to the gym, I could see she thinks I'm desperate. I am not desperate; I'm out of practice.

Jack stopped by my office on the way out. I thanked him for the chocolate. He smiled and said it was his pleasure. I thought another invitation might be offered, but in the end, he just left, saying "Have a great night!"

I'd have a better night if part of it was at a movie or hanging out with my good-looking boss.

As I grabbed my things, my phone went off. I thought I was getting a call, but it was an alarm I set last week when this whole thing started. I'd completely forgotten that I have a date with, um, someone. Oh my gosh, I forgot his name, Brad's friend or cousin or something. What is his name?

I'd left myself a note to meet him downtown at El Bistro at 7:00. I've been wanting to go there forever, but I couldn't find anyone who'd go with me. It is expensive, especially for a Mexican place. Now before you accuse me of being mercenary, I didn't pick the place; he did, What's-His-

Name.

I arrived exactly on time for my date. The hostess directed me to a table by the window. This guy stood when I walked up. It was like I'd just stepped into a black and white movie. He helped me with my chair and said it was nice to meet me. And he is good-looking. Not so drop dead gorgeous that he's prettier than I am, but still easy on the eyes and as I've noted, gentlemanly.

Right at the beginning I should have told him that I forgot his name, but I was embarrassed. He remembered mine and used it throughout the evening. I think he might be Italian. Usually the name is a tip-off. He looks Italian. He owns a deli, which seemed like a great idea, innovative, in our part of the country. He was planning to franchise eventually. He expressed appreciation for non-profits, although he didn't try to delve into what I actually do.

It was a very nice first date.   And it will be our last.

Now, I would love to blame this on some big thing that happened. I don't think he noticed that I never called him by his name even once, but maybe it made me act more awkwardly than I usually would. There was not a lot of chemistry there. He was a little on the distant side anyway, but we could have gotten past that, I think, on future dates if he hadn't forgotten his wallet.

Yes, I once again paid for a date, only this time I had to pay for his meal, too, and let me tell you it was not cheap.

He was mortified. He was not just embarrassed; he was slide under the table, wish I were dead, oh how could this happen to me mortified.

I assured him, as I dropped my credit card on the plate, that I was fine with it. He said several times that he'd pay me back. I tried to let him know that it could happen to anyone. If he'd just laughed about it, and agreed, instead of making such a big deal about how he never did things like this it could have just been a funny memory that we would tell our nice-mannered, good-looking Italian children about some day.

But no, he was too proud. He walked me to my car and disappeared into the night like Darkwing Duck. I guess it was for the best. Someone who has such ridiculously high expectations of himself would have the same unreachable expectations of me and our cute Italian kids some day. But other than the pride thing, he seemed to be a great guy.

So Date Number Four ended with me going home early. Well, I have to get up for work tomorrow anyway, so it's just as well.

Grace was surprised when I walked through the door so early. She was lying on the couch when I came in, but sat up and paid attention when I told her about my date. Then she looked thoughtful, like trying to decide if she should say something. What she said kind of shocked me a little.

"I think you two are a bit too much alike," she said lightly. She talks like that when she wants to let me down easy. She is usually sisterly and blunt, and often kids around with me. A girl needs someone in her life like a sister who will lay it on the line. Of course, she's my younger sister, so she's not always right.

"I agree; we were kind of like two magnets that have the same polarization; so we repel each other. There wasn't any chemistry there."

"No, I meant more like two proud people who aren't willing to admit they could make a mistake."

Now I am the first person to admit my mistakes, and I told my little sister so.

"See how you just called me 'little sister'? You did that so you could totally write off what I said without having to apply it to your life. Why didn't you just tell him at the beginning that you forgot his name?"

"It was just an awkward situation. I'm not proud. I confess my mistakes all over the place. For instance, I spill my guts all the time in my blog."

"You mean the blog where you're going by an alias like a criminal?"

A criminal? Really? I'm using pseudonyms to protect people like her from looking bad. I couldn't believe she called me that.

I'm going to bed. Good night.

* * *

You know how sometimes when you go to bed thinking about something, you wake up and everything is clear? That happened to me this morning.

Grace is right. I am proud. Why didn't I accept that I'd forgotten his name? It was a simple mistake, less monumental than forgetting a wallet. But I made a big deal about the fact that he wouldn't let that wallet thing go.

Now before you write me and tell me that pride is a good thing, please note that there are two kinds of pride. There is the self-respecting kind that takes pride in doing your job ethically and taking enough care of your appearance so you don't look like a bag lady, etc. But the other kind just says to people, "Look at me. Look how well I'm doing." Doesn't that ultimately push people away? Because they can never reach the heights that you have? It never occurred to me that I was doing that. I was just trying to do what I was supposed to do. Live right, walk straight. I am a Christian after all.

And I know Christianity isn't just about doing the right thing. It's about a relationship with Jesus. But hey, it's also about doing the right thing, living in a way that pleases God. I didn't think my pride could be getting in the way of that. If anything, I thought it helped me to live a godly life. I may have been wrong.

I was thinking about this when I arrived at work today, so at first I didn't see that I was greeted with a beautiful bouquet of a dozen red roses. They were placed front and center on my desk. Now, I will tell you, I was surprised. Jack must have shelled out a lot of moolah for these. I didn't think we had reached a place in our relationship that he would buy something that expensive for me. I mean a bag of chocolate is one thing. A boss could (and perhaps even should) dole out good chocolate on a regular basis, but these flowers signified deeper feelings. Should I be dating other people? Were we that serious? I was actually a little embarrassed. The other people in the office were going to think we had a full-blown love affair going on if he was giving me red roses. I looked around for a place to put them so they wouldn't be so noticeable.

But wouldn't that be rude? Jack had spent too much money on these for me to stick them back in the corner of my credenza. Anyway, we hadn't done anything wrong. We had lunch once. Plus, no one would even know they were from him.

I would just enjoy the flowers. They were lovely and smelled wonderful. I took a big whiff again just to get his money's worth. Zoe came in.

"What lovely flowers! Who are they from?" she asked.

I should have known that someone would ask that, and of course that person would be Zoe, the biggest mouth in the place. Was it really any of her business?

"They are beautiful, aren't they?" I said. Sometimes the best answer is to just nonchalantly not answer a question. Then people go on to something else.

"Who sent them?"

Figures I couldn't get off that easily. Then I had an idea. "A secret admirer," I said mysteriously.

Zoe smelled them. "Mmm, just beautiful."

She turned to go. Just then Jack walked in. "How do you like the flowers?" he asked.

Zoe looked confused at first; then she slid out and headed for her desk. I saw her pick up her phone. If I wasn't wearing spiked heels, I would have kicked myself. Why did I say that?

I thanked Jack for the lovely flowers. He smelled them, smiled, and then he continued on to his office.

Was the guy ever going to ask me out again? Isn't it kind of sending a mixed message to give someone gifts, but not continue a relationship?

I went out to Zoe at the front desk. When I walked up, she hung up the phone and started typing or at least pretended to type.

"Uh, Zoe, I was just kidding about that whole secret admirer thing. The flowers are just a thank you gift from Jack."

She raised her eyebrows when I said "thank you gift."

"I mean to thank me for helping him acclimate as manager here," I said quickly.

She nodded. I think I just made it worse, if that was possible. As I went back into my office, I saw her pick up the phone again. I moved the flowers to the back corner of my credenza.

I stared at the bouquet for a moment. Why did he give me these? It's got to be as some kind of thank you gift. He probably doesn't realize that red roses mean something that another color, say yellow, do not.

Whatever he feels, he hasn't said anything outright. I'm going to keep going on my blind dates. They are harmless, after all.

Chapter Seven

Trent and I had agreed to continue our Quest to Test last night. This restaurant was one of the pricier options in the Asian category, in our town at least. We'd been saving this place until we both had the extra cash. It was a quality establishment. No cat served there for sure!

Please don't write me and tell me all of the reasons why I shouldn't have said that. I'm only joking, and it's America after all. Whatever happened to free speech?

We didn't end up eating there anyway. My phone rang as soon as we were seated. It was Ruth.

"Where are you?" she said.

I named the restaurant.

She said, "Why are you there?"

"I was thinking of redoing our decor in Chinese, and I'm trying to get some ideas."

"What?"

"I'm eating of course. What do you do at restaurants?"

"I meant why are you there instead of here," she said.

She was taking way too long to make her point. "What are you talking about, Ruth?"

"You're missing the family reunion!"

Oops. "I've been busy lately, Ruth. I completely forgot about the reunion."

"I suppose it's all of these dates you've been going on. You're such a social butterfly nowadays. Well, it's already started, so hurry. It's at Mom's and Dad's house."

I've barely dated! I've been on like three or four blind dates, for goodness sake. I tossed my phone in my purse. "I'm sorry, Trent. I'm going to have to bail on you. I hate to do that to people."

"Family reunion tonight?" he asked.

"Yes. I can't believe I forgot it. I wonder if Aunt Liz made her pretzel salad."

"It isn't a reunion without Aunt Liz's pretzel salad," he said.

I laughed. We walked out together, and I was just about to drive away when I remembered Trent had ridden there with me. Now I was going to be even later giving him a ride back to his car.

"How about I just come with you? I've never had pretzel salad," Trent said.

That was just about the worst idea known to man. It must have shown on my face.

"No? You're pretty stingy with the salad. Never mind, I'll call someone for a ride." He pulled out his phone.

"It's just that if you come with me, everyone will assume you're with me," I said.

"That's usually how it works," he said.

"No, I mean people will assume we're together."

"That's usually how it works," he said again.

"No, I mean they'll think we're *together*."

"Oh, I see; I don't want to make trouble with your family." He called someone, but it went to voicemail. I sighed. I guess I owed him. He'd rescued me so many times, and he really seemed to want to go. Probably because he doesn't have a big family. They aren't very close either.

I grabbed his arm. "Okay, but let's hurry before all of the good stuff is gone."

* * *

It was worse than I feared. I swear half of my relatives are deaf and the other half clueless. I don't know how many people I had to tell that Trent was just a friend, at a decibel level that should have informed the

78

whole gang. Someone was playing Frank Sinatra music too loudly in the background. We're not related to him, so I'm not sure why they felt like his presence was required.

You'd think the grapevine, which is usually in full swing, would have kicked in sometime during the evening. I introduced Trent to every person there as my friend. "Boyfriend?" was usually the next word to come out their mouths. Sometimes said hopefully, sometimes puzzled, which was just insulting for somebody. I'm not sure who.

Great Aunt Tilly was the worst. She never got it. "I'm so proud of you," she said to me several times. Then she patted his arm. "She likes cake."

"We were just heading that way now, Aunt Tilly." We quickly left and got in line for the buffet.

This was a true potluck dinner. At Nordstrom family reunions you were expected to bring homemade food. You'd never live it down if you didn't. Dare to bring "store-bought" potato salad, and all of the aunts would gather in the corner and whisper about you. They were still talking about the cookie scandal of 2012 when I brought a package of E.L. Fudge. This time I'd stopped for potato chips. They were allowed for some unknown reason. I don't make the rules.

There were so many people there that the party overflowed to the backyard. My parents' terrier, Twister (named for his odd propensity for twirling), was doing his usual job of going from person to person begging for whatever food was left on their plates. Since we were late, I was in a sweat that there wouldn't be any food left for us. Fortunately, there was plenty, even pretzel salad. I'm not sure what Trent was expecting, but he loved it, of course. What's not to love about strawberries, cream cheese, and pretzels?

Things were going along pretty well right about then. I'd introduced Trent to everyone finally. He and I immediately got back in line for seconds on the pretzel salad, scooping up the last bit. We even found a spot at a table.

Twister happened by. I saw it as my chance to unload Aunt Maud's horrible Swedish meatballs without her noticing. They were usually good, but this batch had too much mace in them. I secretly slipped Twister the meatball when I was sure Maud wasn't looking.

That's when Aunt Trudy arrived. It got totally quiet all of a sudden. You could have heard a sock drop. The aunts all gathered in the corner to gossip in a stage whisper.

Every family has its black sheep; ours might have more than the normal allotment. Aunt Trudy fits the category not only for her avoidance of family and her snarky manner, but also because she'd managed to tick off a third of the family in one fell swoop. When her daughter got married, she opted for a very small, very tasteful reception at one of the pricier places in town. This meant she couldn't invite everyone. I wasn't invited, and I didn't care, but many in the family took it as a huge slap in the face.

I was wondering who dropped the ball and clued her in on the event tonight. I could see that everyone was looking around, wondering the same thing. If I were Trudy, watching everyone watch me walk up to the buffet table, gripping a Chinet plate in my sweaty hands like nothing had happened, I wouldn't have been able to stand the pressure. People grabbed their children and moved to the side like it was the Hatfields and the McCoys and gun blasts would erupt any second. Except our feud was Trudy and her son Chase against almost everyone else.

Then Great Aunt Tilly walked over to Trudy and hugged her. That made sense, since Trudy was her daughter. Tilly must have been the one who invited her. But then Tilly asked where Bill was. Trudy and Bill have been divorced for at least five years. For some inexplicable reason, that seemed to restore order to the night. Kind of like, "Tilly's off her rocker; all's right with the world." People gathered and talked again, although no one was talking to Trudy.

Now here is where she might have eaten a quick plate of food and a piece of coconut cream pie and slipped quietly away with Franky crooning her exit music. Chase, her son, who has never been accused of being diplomatic, didn't understand how things work at family reunions, though.

"What's the matter with all of you?" he asked loudly. He didn't seem to have any trouble being heard, maybe because everyone got quiet again. "So what if Mom didn't invite most of you to the wedding. It saved you having to buy Juliet a present."

Uncle Fred exploded in laughter until his wife elbowed him in his ample stomach. He stopped then, but I could see he was turning red from holding it in.

We were back to the awkward silence again, except for Frank singing about the moon in the background. That's when Trent did the medieval knight thing. He put down his plate (and there was still some pretzel salad left on it!), walked over to Trudy, bowed, and said, "May I have this dance?"

She was a little stunned for a second, then she set down her plate, and let him lead her to a grassy spot under a big oak tree near the speakers. They danced for a few minutes, talking quietly, until everyone else went about their business. A few couples even followed their lead and danced, too.

Twister chose that moment to run among the couples, rolling my castaway meatball with his nose. I could feel Aunt Maud looking at me. I pretended I didn't see Twister or the evidence.

After Trent rejoined me, Aunt Tilly came by and said "I'm proud of you," to Trent. He gave her a hug, and she wandered away to sway by herself to the music.

"I'm proud of you, too, Trent," I said. "That was chivalrous, quite a sacrifice for you to do that for my family."

He shrugged. "It wasn't that big of a deal," he said.

"Well, it kind of was. While you were up there, Twister ate your pretzel salad."

Chapter Eight

One of you thinks Jack is going too fast, giving me flowers and chocolate. It probably just seems that way since I'm trying to keep these blog posts relatively short, so I'm not giving the details that would let you know how innocent this is. Really, this relationship hasn't moved along very far at all.

And please don't tell me again how Trent is quite a catch. He's a great friend, but that's all.

So I went on another date two nights ago. I'm sure you're dying to hear about it. Unfortunately, there's not much to tell. I wouldn't exactly call this date a success. John set me up again. This time with a guy from his church, so right off the bat I knew he shared my faith. That was all we shared. I think. Hard to say when I basically had a running conversation with myself all night. That's all you need to hear about this date.

When I got home, I told Grace about the guy. She said, "I thought you might like the strong, silent type."

"Grace, he could have been a mute for all I know." Seriously.

"I know a guy who won't shut up that I could fix you up with," she said. She wasn't kidding either.

So next I had a day that made the quiet guy seem like a dream date. Yes, I said "day" not "date." Grace set me up this time. It wasn't the chatty guy she knew. It was a guy from work, Kevin, that she thought would be perfect for me. The athletic, outdoorsy type. In case you haven't caught on, I am anything but athletic or outdoorsy. She thought he'd be good for me because he'd stretch me. Actually the opposite happened.

Okay, first he's quite muscular; they usually are when they're athletes. Second, he was handsome and gentlemanly. So when he picked me up (not literally although I'm pretty sure he could with no trouble), I'd like to think he's the kind of guy who would open a car door for a girl, but that wasn't possible since his car had no doors. It was a Jeep.

While I've seen Jeeps without doors, I figured that they were for those who are slightly insane. Well, if that's what it takes, I've officially flipped. In fact, when we pulled up to a traffic light, the middle-aged woman next to me looked at me like I'd have to be nuts to drive around in a vehicle like that, about to face plant on concrete. Okay, I'm exaggerating... I wore my seatbelt, so it would have been hard to fall out. It just felt like I was falling out, especially since he took corners on two wheels and considered traffic lights suggestions. My head felt woozy.

Unfortunately, that was the safest I felt all day. On our way to "The Event" it occurred to Kevin that I might be hungry. He's very considerate. So he asked, "Do you like Mexican food?"

Well, of course I like Mexican food; who doesn't? But where does he take me? It was a little hole in the wall that has "the best tortillas." That's like going to a breakfast place because they have the best toast. The place was a total turnoff. I personally couldn't get beyond the weird machinery assembly line that made the tortillas. It looked like it was invented in the bronze age.

No, I'm kidding. Actually it was run by bicycle gears, but that's just primitive and oily enough to be off-putting in a restaurant. Kind of took away my appetite, but I made myself eat the thing he ordered for me. "The House Special" he called it. I couldn't pronounce it, but it got spicier the more I ate. It had a lot of green things in it, too.

My stomach was screaming "Tums!" by the time we left. It didn't help that we got back in the Jeep and rushed off like he was a stunt car driver who was late for a shoot. Maybe he was. Between my sick stomach and woozy head, I was in no shape to remember the man's occupation.

I knew I didn't have any antacids in my purse, and I didn't want to look like a wimp, so I suggested we stop for ice cream. Ice cream is universal and would soothe my stomach. Even weightlifters eat it, right?

Not this weightlifter. He graciously obliged me and my sweet tooth, though, and stopped to get me a mint chip double dip cone. I barely got in two licks before he screeched out of the parking lot and presto chango, I was wearing two dips of mint chip ice cream.

He didn't notice, so I shook the scoops onto the ground, bid them a sad goodbye, and had to make due with nibbling on the cone. It didn't help calm my stomach, of course, but at least I saved face. Oh, we always have to save face on a blind date, don't we? I think that is Rule Number One.

Well, we went roaring off to "The Event." I'm sure you've figured out by now that the next part of the date went south. Funny term, "went south" because that's pretty much what happened literally.

So we arrived at "Daredevil Spelunkers." Yes, I made that up. I forgot what the group was called. I think it was the name of some superhero and "spelunkers." Maybe it was Batman. That would at least make sense. But they're all daredevils, so they might as well call themselves by their real names.

Oh Kevin was high-fiving everyone and having a good old time before we even set foot in the cave, but once we got inside he was in his element. In case you didn't realize what a spelunker is, I believe the dictionary definition is people with bats in their belfry who get their jollies walking, crawling, falling etc. inside caves... probably to visit other bats.

Did I say falling? Yes, they don't even mind falling, just so long as they can be inside a scary, dark, damp, guano-filled space. If you don't know what guano is, I'll save you the trouble of looking it up. It's Spanish for "Oh great, what did I just step in?"

If I had a dime for every time some yelled "To the Bat Cave!" and laughed hysterically, I could have paid for a new pair of jeans to replace the ones that ripped when I slid down what Kevin called an incline, but I called a hole. That was the going south part. I'm still not sure how that happened. I was wearing my miner's helmet or whatever they call it. I had a flashlight at some point, too. That disappeared. I must have dropped it in the hole. Well, now the next sucker, I mean spelunker, can use it when she falls in.

Funny thing about holes... they always seem to be filled with water. This one was not the exception. I'm guessing there was a fair amount of mud or something in there too. Okay, sure, it was probably bat guano! Thanks for making me admit that!

Well, mud or guano or whatever it was, it was very slippery. Kevin finally had to slide down the "incline" and push me up. Yes, it was just about the most embarrassing thing that has ever happened to me.

You're probably thinking, "What's the big deal, Annika? Kevin's strong; he can handle it, and it's dark in a cave. No one could see your heiney being boosted up." Wrong, you forgot about the Daredevil Spelunkers. They wouldn't abandon one of their own. They all gathered around the hole and shined their miner's helmets on me. Gee thanks for the show of solidarity guys, but I'd rather not share my wet, guano-coated rescue with 20 strangers. If you look on Youtube, you can probably find a clip of it.

Okay, call me a downer, but I was ready to leave after that mishap. Kevin wanted to keep going. (Of course! It was just getting fun!) I told him to go ahead; I could find my own way out. His mistake was believing me.

Yeah, I was wrong. Very wrong. I couldn't find the way out. In fact, I think I went the exact opposite direction of the exit/entrance. I came to a fork that didn't look familiar, so what did I do? I took it!

Now you may very well be thinking I deserved what came next, but honestly, does stupidity really necessitate calamity? I mean, I believe in consequences for actions as much as the next girl, but really, does getting stuck in a cave opening seem fair? You know how it goes, though. You walk on through the cave and the passage narrows, but you've invested a lot of time on this particular route. What are you supposed to do? Go back? No way! You press on, until finally you're crawling on all fours, squeezing through something that in the light of your miner's helmet looks big enough to fit through. Alas, it was not.

If any of you are thinking of Winnie-the-Pooh and how he got stuck right after lunch, all I can say is that is not true, and highly insulting. But it is possible that wet jeans are not the best thing to wear when trying to pass through tight spaces. And maybe it's not a good idea to go off by yourself in a cave.

So I had to crouch there scrunched in that cave and yell and whistle until I finally heard someone say, "Hey, Kevin, I think your girlfriend's stuck again."

I could hear him muttering that I wasn't his girlfriend, but he and the other daredevils all came back with their miner's helmets and somehow got me pushed back. We left after that.

When I emerged into the sunlight I would have kissed the ground except that's overly dramatic and disgusting. I was very happy to have lived through the experience even though I couldn't actually see after being in a cave so long. Now I know how the poor bats feel.

Kevin borrowed a garbage bag from someone for me to sit on, but I could see he wasn't excited about driving me anywhere. If you thought he drove fast before, that was nothing compared to how fast he could go when he had a reason to drive at breakneck speed. And he was on a mission.

So you see, although I considered blind dates to be fairly benign, I was all wrong. They can be very dangerous.

And watch your step in caves!

Chapter Nine

Now someone is worried about my safety. Honestly, I was never actually in any danger. I didn't fall far at all into the hole in the cave. Crazycatlady is such a worrywart.

Okay, so the cave wasn't the best date I've ever been on. So what? I lived. On to the next one, which is tonight. Now this guy, Jonah, is someone else that John knows. I don't remember how John knows him, but he said he's quite a popular guy. I'm not into popularity, but maybe John just means that he's friendly. I'll let you know what he's like.

In the meantime, let me tell you what's been happening with Grace. She's going out on a date with someone. Now I know she was kidding me about never dating, but she really never dates. She hasn't brought him home to meet us, yet, so I'm kind of wondering why not. She must think we won't like him.

She mentioned it in passing at a painting party the family was having. John had recently moved into a different apartment. In addition to switching jobs often, John moves almost every year. There's always a better apartment on the horizon, don't you know. It's either newer, better neighbors, or closer to work, although I don't know why he bothers with that last one as the reason when he knows he'll just be moving on to another job soon, anyway.

The last apartment he moved into needed work. Either someone played baseball in there or they'd been putting their fist through the wall regularly. After John patched the many holes in the walls, he invited us all over to help cover them with the same boring white he always uses. John got in the habit of painting every surface white. Maybe he does it because he's always on the verge of moving out, and since some landlords require walls be left that color, he just saves hauling us all over for another painting party.

When Grace sprung it on everybody that she was dating someone I was out picking up pizza. She'd left by the time I got there. When she said no one there knew him, they didn't bother to ask his name.

In the meantime, I have to get ready to go out with Jonah. It's so hard to know what to wear for these dates. I never know where we're going, so it's hard to know if I'm overdressing. I decided at some point to just have fun and not worry about it. John said I didn't need to dress up, but guys always say that.

I'll write you later about what happened.

* * *

Jonah is very good looking. Maybe he's too good looking. He came up to the door and was introduced to Grace. When he turned around to open the door when it was time to leave she was making all kinds of gestures and faces that meant she thought he was gorgeous. Well that made me a little self-conscious because I'm not exactly dazzling. I don't mind. I like the way I look in spite of my crazy hair. He even told me I looked very pretty. I did get dressed up for this one. Good thing I didn't listen to John. Never listen to your brother on matters of dress. (Unless he's advising more modesty. Definitely listen to him then!)

We went to a rather lavish restaurant. It was perfect for talking, with soft music in the background. It was nice not to have to yell over the music for once. We were sitting there enjoying our steaks when all of a sudden a leggy blond walks up and starts talking to him. She was mad. It was very awkward until he took her outside. When he came back, he said she didn't realize they had broken up. I didn't know how someone couldn't understand that, but at least he stopped her from making a scene at our table.

You won't believe where he took me afterward... Pets-R-Us! He wouldn't say at first, wanting to surprise me, and it certainly did. Now before you think he was just cheap, let me tell you that it was fun walking

94

around looking at all the different breeds and discussing which ones we liked best. He insisted I hold a particularly sweet little fluff ball that looked lonely all by itself in a cage. For a while I was wondering if Jonah owned stock in the company, but he insisted that he just likes dogs. Well when we were in that little cubicle room, just the two of us and the puppy, he made sure he sat close to me and was petting the dog that was in my arms. It was all a little cozier than I like on a first date, so I suggested we go.

Things started on a downward spin after we left the puppies. He invited me to his apartment, which I thought was a little inappropriate. I did ask him back to our place since I thought Grace was there. When we arrived, though, she was gone! I didn't know how I was going to explain that.

Well, he totally misread the circumstances, because as soon as I sat down, he moved over to sit next to me and kissed me. And when I say kissed, I don't mean like your grandma kisses you. I was about to set him straight when Grace came in. She looked a little shocked to see the two of us necking on the couch, but Jonah and I were even more surprised by what she brought in with her. It was that leggy blond again! She had followed us and slipped inside when Grace arrived!

Leggy Blond just burst right in and lit into him. Seems she really wasn't his ex-girlfriend. She's his present girlfriend, only now she really is his ex after that little trick he pulled. I gathered that when he took her outside at the restaurant that he said I was an old friend of the family or something like that! That he was just taking me out to do a favor for his sister! Of all the nerve!

Well, she slapped him, broke up with him, and left. He had the good sense to leave immediately after she did. Maybe the looks on Grace's face and mine were clues that he wasn't going to fare any better with us than he did with her.

I wasted no time letting Grace know that this was not a mutual thing. I had no trouble convincing her. I'd meant to ask when she got home who she'd been out with, but I completely forgot when Jonah's ex swept in.

So be warned and learn from my experience. Watch out for wolves in sheep's clothing (or rather players pretending to be dog lovers).

Chapter Ten

Grace was a little vague when I asked her where she was last night. I'm starting to worry about her. We've never kept secrets from each other. I hate to press her into telling me, but why would she hide it? She said she'd been out with a group of people, so I let it drop.

I know some of you are going to love it when you hear about my last date. Some of you will say meh, and others of you will commiserate with me. I went horseback riding with Christopher.

Now those of you who know what you're doing on the north end of a horse are right now envisioning a beautiful, peaceful ride through the countryside, maybe just at sunset, but definitely a relaxing, enjoyable experience. Those of you who aren't into that sort of thing are probably just saying, "Why does Annika keep making a big deal out of everything? So she rode a horse, so what?" But some of you know that when I say horseback riding I mean that giant, scary animal that you can't climb onto, you can't straddle, and you can't stay seated on because it wants you off!

At least that was what "Buttercup" seemed to be saying to me. "Get off human. Chris may not be wise to you, but you and I both know that you don't know what you're doing." I decided that whoever named

Buttercup must have done it as a joke. There couldn't be a grumpier horse, and she reminds no one of a flower.

Christopher knows how to ride; he's a natural. He dresses the part, too, and does it well. I looked and rode like an amateur. And when I use the term "rode," I do it loosely.

Chris made it sound like fun, but those horses are a lot higher when you actually get up on them than they look from below. Buttercup kind of pawed the ground and moved around as soon as I was helped onto her back. She put up with me on there, or rather she bided her time until we were out of sight of the barn; then she threw me.

Now I don't know if she felt guilty for tossing me so promptly on the ground or if my guardian angels are working overtime since I started going on all of these dates, but Buttercup threw me on a heaping stack of straw. Then she ran off.

Sure, I got up, brushed myself off, and figured I'd just get back on. That's what they always say, right? "When you get thrown, you get right back on a horse." A couple of things wrong with that... one, I can't get up on the beast without help, and two, Buttercup had other plans.

Just finding her was a chore. Then I tried to get back on, but she kept going around in a circle. I kind of flung myself over sideways and was thrown again. I decided to respect her wishes after that and hiked back to the barn. I would have led her back with me, but she suddenly turned into a mule when I tried to lead her and planted her feet, not budging. She did everything but bray!

None of this should have interfered with getting to know Chris, right? Oh you are so wrong. It turns out that Buttercup is Chris's baby. He loves that horse. He only let me ride her as a favor to me. Yes, he's the one that named her that, and it wasn't done as a joke. He meant it. But you should see her with him. It's like she's his faithful dog, very affectionate. I just couldn't come between the two of them, and you'd know if you looked her in the eye, that she had no intention of letting me.

So long, Christopher, you and Buttercup ride off into the sunset of my blog while I pick straw out of my hair. I just realized what I did wrong. The saying isn't "If you get thrown, get back on a horse." It's "If you fall off of a horse, get right back on." You'd have to be out of your tree to try to get back on a horse that threw you when you don't even know how to ride.

Have you noticed a pattern; how the concept of "crazy" keeps coming up? Honestly, I never thought of myself as daft before this experiment began. But all of these blind dates must be affecting me that way.

And now someone has suggested I bring a bike helmet on dates. Very funny, although I probably could have used one when Buttercup threw me; honestly these dates are not at all dangerous.

This next idea may seem a little outdated, but it was all new to me... karaoke. I'd never done it. Of course this was Elvis's idea, not mine, but then these dates never are, are they?

Blond hair, no sideburns, and initially no twitching lips or hips, so I didn't name him Elvis because he looks like the King or talks like him or reminds me in any way of the Hillbilly Cat... until the music started playing. Then all bets were off.

I thought it was a cute idea - a karaoke contest at a coffee shop. I would've been happy just to observe, but Elvis said watching karaoke but not participating was like watching baseball versus playing it yourself. I could agree, kind of, with my limited knowledge of the game.

But I thought of a better analogy... watching someone else kiss. What fun is that? Well, Elvis gave me some funny, sidelong glances when I said that. It wasn't like I was trying to get the Big El to lay one on me!

The night of the date he didn't dye his hair or wear a rhinestone jumpsuit, but he did slick back his short, blond hair and wear jeans and a button-down shirt with the sleeves rolled up. Maybe he was going for Young Elvis in the 60s. I hadn't thought to wear a costume, just my usual jeans and a light sweater. He didn't suggest I change, but I saw him looking over my outfit when he arrived. Sorry, El, I don't own a mini-skirt, and the bouffant wasn't happening.

On the way over, Elvis played a CD of the song he'd chosen for us to do, (You're the) Devil in Disguise. I'm sure you're wondering as I did, why in the world would he pick that one? Never mind that as the designated recipient of the song he'd be calling me a devil; what was my performance going to entail? Mute angel/she devil? I suggested I just sit out the song. After all, I don't feel the need to take center stage. I would have been perfectly willing to sing backup as one of the Sweet Inspirations. There wasn't a backup woman's part, though in the song he picked, and I thought I'd feel dumb just standing there while he sang and danced around me.

He said we should do this together. I'm not sure why, but since he wanted me to participate, there was no sitting it out for me. Well, right after that, a song came on his cd from the movie Viva Las Vegas, a duet, The Lady Loves Me. Perfect! I was thrilled to do that one instead. Elvis agreed. I looked the lyrics up on my phone, and we practiced it a few times on the way there.

We arrived, got in line, and took a number. Until it was our turn, Elvis alternated between sipping a double espresso with meditating off by himself in a corner. Every time a new act got up, though, he zeroed in on their performance like this was the contest of a lifetime.

I've never claimed to be a singer, but I would have sworn it was impossible for me to be that bad at karaoke. It was so much easier to sing along with Ann-Margret on the cd than to do it by myself. I wish I could say it was a distortion in the speakers somehow. It certainly didn't sound like me. I was kind of off-key and a little off tempo. The audience was pretty forgiving; at least no one threw tomatoes.

Elvis on the other hand was impressive. He sounded like the Big E and had his mannerisms down to the twisting hips and snapping fingers. The man must have been studying The Cat for years. If only he'd done a song by himself where he could shine, like Jailhouse Rock.

But no, he did one with me. I think he regretted it from the first notes that came out of my mouth. He looked startled.

Okay the man was great; I'll give him that. He certainly knew it. He was more like Elvis than Elvis was. Don't ask me how that's possible, but it's true. He totally dripped with arrogance, too. Well, it was actually sweat, which he wiped with a towel and threw into the audience... like someone would take that home as a souvenir!

In the original performance in the movie, the King pulls off the song without being overly contemptible, but this guy seemed to actually believe what he was singing, only it was more universal, like (All of) The Ladies Love Me. By the end of the song I would have gladly pushed him into a pool like Ann-Margaret did to Elvis.

He won. Yay. Notice I didn't say "we won," even though technically I was half of the act. Everyone applauded like mad and crowded around him commenting on how believable he was. I was invisible, so I grabbed a mocha latte and sat back down. He kept saying "Thank you, thank you very much," in his EP voice until I was ready to smack him upside his greasy head except my hand would have just slid off.

This place has a charming custom: winner does an encore, so he got to do The Devil in Disguise after all. He didn't ask me to join him onstage, and I did not volunteer. When it looked like a girl might swoon, I jotted a note on a napkin saying I needed some air, and that I would find my own way home and left.

I know it sounds like I am a spoilsport, but the guy was better off without me. He needs to head to Vegas to follow his true calling as an Elvis impersonator.

* * *

Trent and I made it back to the expensive Asian restaurant tonight that we missed eating at because of my family reunion. We arrived there a little late because first we had to watch my new robot vacuum do her thing. Trent wanted to see her work, so we went through the whole 45-minute cycle. Well, Trent did;   he's easily amused. I spent the time catching up on emails, doing my nails, reading a book...

I don't blame him. I watched her for a while when she first arrived. Have you ever noticed how fascinating these machines are in spite of their snarky manner? Almost hypnotizing. Eventually her rudeness got to me. When I remove the dirt collector, she says in a judging tone, "Please replace the dust bin." Dust bin? Is this vac from the UK? Because she doesn't have an English accent, although I think I'd like her better if she did. And how does she expect me to empty it unless I remove it?

The vacuum is definitely a she, a fastidious cleaner with a high pitched voice. And what an attitude! If you don't get out of the way, she runs into you. Kind of like "What? You wanted me to clean, right?" Also, she's always ringing out with loud, obnoxious tones to get my attention before she chews me out. "Ding, ding, ding - wheel overload!" whatever that means and "Ding, ding, ding - please put the machine in a safe place!"

after she gets stuck like she hadn't done it to herself. I'll admit I talk back, maybe because her tone is so high and mighty. "Ding, ding, ding, please don't wedge yourself under the furniture!"

Fortunately, we didn't have reservations, since Trent simply couldn't tear himself away from Gertrude. That's my vacuum's name. She reminds me of my Aunt Trudy whose real name is Gertrude. I think Aunt Tilly must have still been under anesthesia when she chose that name. I know you're thinking "What's your excuse, Annika?" but honestly the name fits this vac.

Anyway, we eventually arrived at the restaurant after Gertrude parked herself, and Trent got to see the amazing amount of dirt she collected in her dust bin. Good times.

We were seated in the Land that Time Forgot. Seriously, have you ever noticed there is a certain time of day when the restaurant looks suitably empty, and you'd think that service would be quick, but all of the wait staff suddenly disappear? I've heard people say they're probably doing their side work, but I'm convinced they have a poker game going on in the kitchen. They're probably crowded around the prep table betting with cucumber slices and only emerge when one of them runs short on tips and has to bus a table to ante up.

So we had to wait to order, were given cold appetizers, lukewarm entrees, and no silverware except chopsticks. I've never been good with those things. Trent said new experiences were good for me. He seemed to find it amusing to watch me balance and drop every bite on the plate. I didn't find it quite so amusing, especially after my shrimp fell off and rolled under the table. I'd been waiting so long at home on Gertrude that I was absolutely starving by the time we got to the restaurant.

We finally decided to just take it home and reheat it in the microwave, since the server hadn't appeared so we could let her know about the tepid food. But no one would come out to give us our check and some to go boxes. I suggested leaving the food without paying since we'd only nibbled anyway, but Trent wouldn't hear of it. Right then an Asian woman that I assumed was the manager walked by. I said, "Excuse me, could we get our check, please?"

She narrowed her eyes and said, "I wouldn't know since I don't work here!" and walked into the restroom.

In my defense, she was dressed like a manager - blue pants and a white button down shirt. Anyway, I couldn't think clearly with so little food in my stomach.

I grabbed a couple of to go boxes from under the cash register, and we dropped enough cash on the table to cover our meals and the tax. Trent also left enough for a modest tip. I tried to argue him out of that, pointing out tips were supposed to be a reward for good service and besides, he was only supporting her gambling habit. He left the money anyway.

I swear when we walked by the kitchen I heard someone say, "Dealer takes four," but Trent didn't hear a thing.

Chapter Eleven

Remember how Will's dog tagged along on my first ever blind date? Grace even thought Will brought another person along. Well, last night's date actually did that! Dylan brought Jason, a second cousin twice removed or something. Let's just call him a distant cousin. They both were relatively good-looking, but that's where any similarity ended. And Zoe seriously owes me one after last night.

Other than not wanting to be alone with me, Dylan had another problem, a big one. On some of these dates, I've been the problem, at least partially. But this guy was the epitome of what happens when you single out an entire sex and expect them to shoulder the blame for all of the problems of the world: A.K.A. female-bashing or conversely male-bashing.

Let's start with Dylan pulling into the driveway and sitting there... just sitting! After ten minutes, I wondered if I should charge him a fee to park as it looked like he was going to be there all night. Maybe the next step would be him honking the horn. It definitely wasn't going to be me running out to the car. Eventually he came to the door, said who he was, and we walked out together. Does the guy think it's degrading to walk up to a door for someone?

Next, Dylan called me by the wrong name all night. That felt disrespectful. And don't write me and tell me that Annika is a difficult name to remember. That is not my real name! It was more like someone saying Diane instead of Diana. I know that's not a huge deal, but I did correct him several times. I was starting to wonder if he was doing it on purpose to be funny. It wasn't, by the way. Even Jason could remember it and corrected Dylan. Eventually he stopped calling me anything.

Oh, but he did call me all kinds of things by proxy. From the "woman driver" who cut him off, to the waitress who fell on the "ditzy" side of the coin, the man just had nothing nice to say about females... any females. He lightly peppered the meal with comments that were alternately condescending and outright insulting. Neither of which was particularly flattering for either of us. Woman-bashing does not make you look smart; in fact it's just the opposite.

The condescension was there while we ordered. I looked over the menu and asked what calamari was; Dylan rolled his eyes. I'm not well-versed in exotic seafood. I can live with that; what I didn't need was the show of contempt.

Jason on the other hand was an easy-going guy and was very complimentary not only to women in general, but also to me specifically.

He admitted that he was not very good with figures and admired someone (me) who could handle them with ease. When Dylan heard I was an accountant, his eyes glazed over.

I get that kind of reaction a lot from people when I say what I do, so I don't blame him on that one, except his was exceptionally rude. Now I don't expect people to applaud when I walk into a room, but a man can throw a little admiration my way, and I won't resent it. I'm talking sincere compliments, here, not empty flattery.

Jason also said I looked nice when I first got into the car. I thought at the time he was just being kind because he somehow knew Dylan didn't say anything. Maybe the guy had a sixth sense where his cousin was concerned, because Dylan barely looked at me all evening. Maybe the few extra pounds I am carrying insult his idea of what a woman should look like to please him.

After we ate, I thought that would be the end of the date. It was obvious Dylan and I didn't hit it off. He even seemed reluctant to pay the check, letting it sit there on the table for quite a while before pulling out his credit card. It was long after Jason had already paid his. Did Dylan expect me to pay my part? Hey, if that was the way he rolled, I would have been glad to contribute. I'm always careful to order something that isn't pricey anyway.

After dessert, Jason suggested we all go bowling. Dylan didn't look like he was thrilled with the idea until Jason offered to pay for it. Then he was all over it. Of course the best part for Dylan was going to be showing how superior men were at bowling.

I might not be the best athlete, but I can bowl. My family is big on bowling, starting all children out as soon as they can toddle up to the foul line. My form is pretty good, if I do say so myself. Jason and I had a near tie. (I beat him by less than ten points.) The important thing is that we both beat the socks off Dylan. He blamed everything from the ball to the poor lighting to the warped lane. I can't tell you how much I wanted to point out to Dylan that a woman beat him using the same lighting and the same lane... and a lighter ball. I refrained. Shows my great restraint? Right? Well, since this is anonymous, I'll tell you the whole story, even the part I'm not proud of.

I'd never been to this particular downtown bowling alley, so I was a little confused on where the restrooms were located. I got turned around a bit and walked into the men's room! Fortunately, it was empty, and I ran out as soon as I saw what I'd done. Unfortunately, Dylan was just going in and saw the whole thing. Yeah, he laughed at me. I could take that. He told Jason about it; we all laughed again. I'm still okay with that. When we got into the car, he couldn't stop bringing it up, though, like I didn't have a brain in my head. Couldn't I read? There was even a picture. Blah, blah, blah, the guy wouldn't let it go. Maybe he was ticked because I beat him at bowling. Jason even told him to lay off. I could see it was going to be a long ride home.

That's when Dylan did it. He laid out his philosophy of dating, which I gather he doesn't do much. The guy has no filter. Brother, some things are just better left unsaid. Such as his belief that the expectation that men should pay for dates was akin to being a lady of the evening! Only he didn't use that term! I was a little freaked out by that, and the next sound that came out of my mouth was a cross between a squawk and a gasp if a person can pull off making both of those sounds at once.

Oh my gosh, I couldn't believe he said that. Then he made it worse, going on to say the only difference was that men didn't benefit from dating! He had nerve, that one, to say something like that within arm's reach of a woman who was already stewing about being told she was a member of the ignorant sex all night.

I slapped down a twenty dollar bill (which more than paid for my meal and my part of the tip) rather than slapping his face and was out of that car at the next stoplight.

Now you probably think the guy would come right back and apologize when he saw how rude he was. But no, he did the opposite, screeching off as soon as the light turned green. Buh bye Dylan, you easily left twenty dollars worth of tire on the pavement.

Well, that was all well and good, standing on principle like that except now I was in the middle of a dark downtown street with no idea where I was. Walking home in spiky heels was not an option, anyway. I was looking around for a street sign, praying, and pulling out my phone to call for a ride, when a couple of guys started walking toward me and calling out.

I won't tell you what they said, but it was along the same vein as Dylan's comments, only scarier. Forget about phoning for a ride, I was just about to call 9-1-1, when a guy came running down the block.

The other two guys took off when they saw the man coming toward us. I was at 9-1- when I realized it was Jason.

To tell the truth, I was never happier to see a near-stranger than I was at that moment. Jason called his brother to pick us up. We stepped into a nearby diner-type restaurant to wait and had coffee while he did the apologizing that Dylan owed me. It sounds like they will be even more distant cousins after this night. However, Jason and I are much closer. We're going out on our own date.

* * *

And now someone has suggested a chaperone again. I wasn't in any danger last night. It just felt dangerous. Lovethisblog! also suggested I shouldn't have gotten out of the car on a dark downtown street. I think we've all learned from my little show of independence that I could have picked better timing for that.

Jason invited me out to a nice dinner and a concert for the next weekend. He said it was to make up for the horrible night with Dylan, and that we could go anywhere I wanted. These dates don't need to be expensive. The important thing is that we are getting to know each other, not to provide me with a chance to eat at a luxurious restaurant. He insisted, so I told him to just pick the place. He chose La Maison de Ooh La La or something. Well, you get the idea. I would never choose to eat there, but he wanted to.

This was the first date that I got really dressed up. A girl doesn't go to a restaurant like that in her everydays. Jason cleaned up nice, too, wearing a suit. I had a little black number I'd been saving for just such an occasion, and Grace offered to do my makeup since I'm always a little conservative in that department.

Jason was late, but that was okay since Grace was putting the finishing touches on my makeup. When he saw me he told me how pretty

I looked. Finally one of my blind dates was working out. Someone was interested in me.

When we walked into La Maison, it fairly oozed extravagance. Tapestries adorned the walls. Rich, brocaded fabric was everywhere. A four-piece string ensemble played quietly in the corner.

Yes it was all quite lovely. Too bad Jason hadn't made reservations so we could have tasted the food. The maitre d' asked us if we would like to wait in case a table came open. We stood there for thirty minutes, but it didn't look like a table would be available in time since the concert would be starting soon. We decided to grab a snack at the concert and eat afterward.

Jason hadn't looked up the venue of the concert, so we got lost and arrived after it started. Slipping in late normally would be only a slight inconvenience, even when dressed to the nines and wearing a pair of shoes that were engineered only for sitting... except the concert was sold out. No, Jason hadn't thought to buy tickets ahead of time. I was starting to see a trend here where our life together would be a series of arriving late and missing important events: weddings, funerals, the kids' open house...

But Jason wasn't giving up that easily. He'd noticed a guy down the block had set up a portable stand and was scalping, I mean selling tickets. We felt very lucky to get his last two tickets at only a 10%

markup... until we got back to the concert and found out the tickets were counterfeit. Of course the guy was gone by the time we returned to where he'd been.

Jason had done a wonderful job of keeping up our spirits throughout the evening, but I guess that was it for him. He looked pretty dejected. I told him that it didn't matter, but right then my stomach growled. Well, I'd tried, but the stomach doesn't lie.

Never fear, in spite of poor planning, we did get supper eventually. Jason found a nearby gas station that had kind of a 50s diner motif going on. A jukebox played songs from the 50s and 60s. We rocked around the clock while munching unusually good chili dogs with raw onions, and the best onion rings I've ever had. The owner gave me a big cheesecloth towel to wear so I wouldn't drip chili on my dress.

I think the place was featured on that Diners, Drive-ins, and Dives show. Anyway, Jason had a good time. I think he has a thing for that kind of place.

Unfortunately, he doesn't have a thing for me, nor me for him. It was a fun date, but that's all it was.

Chapter Twelve

Someone posted that these dates should be vetted better. The reader is still dwelling on Dylan. Okay, the guy has a twisted sense of dating, but how many guys like that do you think I'm going to meet? Chill people!

How many of you can say your dad set you up on a blind date? Well, now I can say it with you, if you're willing to acknowledge it. I finally figured out that people aren't picking out guys they think would be my soul mates. The females prefer ones they would have chosen if they weren't married. The men opt for guys they envy.

In this instance, my dad is a college professor, and he loves sports. It kind of stands to reason that he would choose an athlete, right? Ah but no, my date is just more of a sports buff than my dad, which I didn't think was possible. It's not like my parents don't have a great marriage, but I will say my dad tunes out Mom (and all of us) sometimes when a game is on.

So Martin and I went to a basketball game. Now I'll admit Martin is a few years older than I am. Not so many that it's weird, but enough that he seems a little more mature than some of the guys I've known. For instance, he's not into video games. He likes his games real... very real.

Okay, I'm a good sport (pun intended). I'm willing to give basketball another try even though I hate it. Maybe hate is too strong of a word for something as boring as dribble dribble dribble... shoot. Dribble dribble dribble... shoot.

Martin picked me up at home and we grabbed something at the concession stand on campus. Did I mention it was a college game? Martin is a teacher at the college. I forgot what he teaches, something to do with computers. I'd feel bad for not remembering, but, hey, I remembered his name at least. That's something. Of course I've changed it here for you.

How to describe this date... How about utterly forgettable. He must have thought he was doing a favor for my dad or something. I felt like I was at a college lecture, and a good title would be "How to Bore Your Date." At least all of the music and stomping that went on kept me awake. It would be terrible to appear on the ten o'clock news asleep in the stands.

I had a hot dog and a coke for supper. I should probably point out here that before I started all of this dating, I ate normal food, real meat, vegetables, etc. But when in Rome... so now I've gained a few pounds and my clothes are getting snug. I hadn't figured on that being a consequence of the experiment. You just never know what is going to happen when you decide to change your life. I think I'd like to change that part back, because the pounds are sticking around.

Anyway, we parted friends, Martin and I, but we definitely parted.

I finally asked Grace who she's been hanging out with lately. She said it was just her bunch of friends. She seems to be gone a lot more, though, almost every evening, and she hasn't invited me to go along like she usually would. Of course, I've been dating a lot, so maybe that's the reason, but I haven't been gone every time.

* * *

I'm calling the date I had a few nights ago The Fender Bender Blind Date. I could just stop right there and let your imaginations fill in the details, but I'll save you the trouble. Besides, I'm pretty sure you wouldn't imagine anyone like Jeremy.

First, let me say that this is why I'm doing an anonymous site. Bad things happen, and I could be sued! Especially after that last date. Although to be honest, Jeremy (and again, not his real name, people) would have to have a lot of nerve to sue anybody.

Jeremy is a friend of Zoe. How she got wind of my little experiment, I'll never know. Probably the same way she learns about everything else around the office; she snoops. This is the second guy she's recommended. She's oh for two so far.

So she sets me up with this friend of hers, Jeremy, and we were going out for a nice dinner and a movie. He drove up in a shiny, silver Lexus. I forgot what Zoe said he does for a living, but Jeremy is loaded, obviously. He rushed to open the car door for me. So I thought points for him for being so gentlemanly. Then I caught a glimpse of him admiring himself in the perfect finish, or maybe he was just admiring the car a.k.a. His Baby. In hindsight, maybe his hurry to open the door was because he didn't trust me not to close it gently enough. You know, he could have just had me meet him at the restaurant if he was afraid I'd harm His Baby. Of course, then I would have actually been able to eat.

He regaled me with the merits of the Lexus as we drove. This is not his first time around the park with this make and model, oh no. Practically all he's ever owned has been the Lexus, so he told me not only the wonderful features of his present car, but also what has changed from his past babies.

Then the fender bender happened. Even though I was his witness, as I have been told many, many times, I didn't see anything. I was staring glassy-eyed out the side window during the Lexus Lecture, and truthfully wouldn't stand up for the guy in court, even if I did see it, even if he was in the right, which I don't know and don't care.

You've never seen anyone throw such a fit about a small scratch. You'd think they'd dropped his baby in a vat of boiling oil laughing gleefully all the while instead of what actually happened, which is some poor schmuck grazed him.

He screamed; he ranted. He called the guy names, really bad ones. I got out of the car when it first happened. When Jeremy started in on the guy, I tried to calm him down and got a nice chunk of a piece of his mind. I got back in the car. I could still hear him, but barely, since the Lexus has wonderful sound-proofing features for which I was much grateful. I would have climbed into the wonderfully padded and roomy back seat to hide from onlookers, but I was afraid of scratching his Moroccan leather with my heels. On second thought, I wish I'd scratched up his seats.

Speaking of heels, Jeremy blessedly stayed outside the whole time to make sure the other guy involved in the accident didn't get away. It was quite a while before the police showed. I would have left, but after being told I was his witness, I was afraid to. I don't need the police hunting me down. Jeremy had mostly calmed down by the time the police arrived, so they didn't know what a jerk he was. I got out of the car when they came. They took me aside privately to get my story, fortunately, so Jeremy can't attach blame to me if his suit gets tossed out of court. When the police said I was done, I got my purse and left. I was wearing the aforementioned high heels, but I would have walked 60 miles in high heels rather than get back in the car and hear Jeremy's story again. I don't think he even noticed when I left. I could have called Grace for a ride, but she was out with friends, so I didn't want to bother her, and it wasn't that far.

I've lost count of what date I was on, but I had PBJ for supper, so does this count as a date anyway?

* * *

I'm surprised how many of you there are now. But I'm grateful for each one of you. It makes doing this more fun when I have so many comments afterward, especially those encouraging me along the way, telling me about the great guys you've met on blind dates. I am not giving up just because I haven't met Mr. Right yet. Jeremy was definitely Mr. Wrong. I do have a few blisters today from walking home in strappy heels, so I wish I phoned for a ride.

On to the next date. This last one was not the most mature guy. I'll tell you right off the bat that he didn't drive a Lexus thankfully. Okay, I'll let it rest about Jeremy. When I told Zoe about Jeremy's rotten temper, she seemed totally surprised, so I guess she didn't know him as well as she thought she did.

You'll never guess how I met this guy. One of my blind dates set us up! I know that sounds a little scary, but isn't it kind of gratifying to know that even though the two of us (Martin and I) weren't meant for each other, he thinks I'm someone he can recommend.

Anyway, the guy showed up in a normal car; we reached the restaurant unscathed, and had a nice meal. Alex is a bit of a show-off, I noticed during the meal. One of those people who exude confidence so much that it gets on your nerves a little. Especially about the things he's confident about. For instance, he seemed to take great pride in his pickiness in ordering, down to the minutiae of what oil was touching his fish. Ever notice how people like that make you want to prove them wrong?

This guy had no intention of taking me to a movie or a play after dinner. No, we went mini-putting. This was perfectly fine with me. Fresh air and something I'm proficient at.

In the nature of full disclosure I felt I had to let Alex know my expertise at mini-golf. My putting is my secret weapon. You wouldn't think to look at this anything but athletic woman that I would be good at something like that involving skill (at anything involving skill), but I know my way around a mini-putt course. When Alex brought it up, I agreed, of course. When I said I was pretty good at it, he seemed to see it as a challenge, taking up the gauntlet as though his honor were at stake, ridiculous as it sounds. This is after all, hitting a little colored ball around a usually waterlogged, unkempt course while something like windmills from the 70s crank around with an elongated squeak that makes you rush to get to the next hole to escape the noise.

This course was no exception. It was supposed to be a take on the Scottish Links of the past... the very distant past. A talking Scottish head with mutton chops and a pipe in his mouth welcomed you to the first hole. The speaker system cut out every other word and kept playing again and again. Hole one was excruciating. I wanted to club the talking head.

Now I don't know the official rules of the place, and I'll allow anyone to move a branch or piece of mulch that was blown or washed onto the course, but Alex went to such great lengths to clear every course that it verged on cheating. Especially since he waited until after my turn to do so. And I started every hole. He acted like he was being gallant. "After you" he would say with a grand sweep of his hand. His gesture didn't fool me for long when he started cleaning the course before my ball stopped rolling.

Okay, I can understand some guys' egos won't let them lose to a slightly plump woman with a desk job. But honestly, was his manhood at stake? I did have three holes-in-one, but I at least played fair. In addition to the cleaning of the course, his spot of the ball when he brought it back in from hitting it out would have been more accurate if he'd closed his eyes and tossed. I kept score, so at least he couldn't cheat that way. If you can't win by skill alone, what does the victory mean?

I will admit that I gloated a little. The guy wasn't that good, though, for all his talk. I know I shouldn't have teased him, but when you hear what happened next, you'll agree that what he did was unforgivable. He left! I beat the guy by a lousy seven points, and while I was in the ladies room, he drove off and left me at Ye Olde Mini-Links!

Yeah, I called my friend Trent for a ride. He's a life-saver, that one. If you're wondering, I've wiped up the course with Trent many times, and he's still speaking to me, so Alex could learn a lesson in humility from Trent.

Chapter Thirteen

Many of you seem to think I owe Trent for bailing me out so often. We practically have a standing Wednesday night for Chinese food. We usually take turns paying, but if I've begged a favor of him that week I always buy. He knows I appreciate his friendship.

If you heard the next guy was a doctor, you'd think I was moving up in the dating hierarchy, wouldn't you? Don't even go there. Doctors may have more money and save people's lives, but they don't make better dates. I had more fun beating Alex, mini-putt guy (well until the end of the date, of course) than my date with Matthew.

I'm not saying every doctor is pompous, and maybe that isn't even the right word for the doc, but what do you call it when a man insists on ordering for you? It wasn't like I had to order in a foreign language. I thought I could find my way around using the English I've spoken since birth. But no. Matthew had to order for both of us. He did it so fast, ordering so many courses, that I had no idea what was coming, except I think the main course was chicken. Maybe.

Besides the ordering for me, there was the foot incident. Right after we (he) ordered, a horrible smell suddenly appeared. I looked around to see what my neighbor had ordered hoping we weren't going to end up with the same thing, but all they had was bread. I finally figured out the smell was emanating from under the table. I sneaked a peek under the tablecloth when Matthew was getting a sip of water, and sure enough, he'd taken off his shoes. I suppose doctors rush around on their rounds, and that could account for sweaty feet, but did he have to share it? I know the waiter even noticed it, because when he dropped off the octopus, a funny look came over his face, and he surreptitiously raised the tablecloth to see the origin of the odor. He did not look pleased when he walked away.

Yes, I did say octopus, by the way. It was an appetizer on little stale crackers with some type of stinky cheese that was vying for worst smell with the feet under the table. I ate it just so I wouldn't have to smell it any longer. A girl can take only so many attacks on her senses. I'll assume at least some of you have never had octopus. Don't bother if it becomes available. It's like the chewy version of the everlasting gobstopper. I chewed it for a long time before I managed to basically swallow it whole. Fortunately, it wasn't a very big piece. Of course, I had a doctor seated across from me, so if I needed the Heimlich performed, he was handy.

Some of you will think this was purely petty of me, and perhaps smelly feet and taking ordering liberties shouldn't have doomed the date.

Yes, but I haven't told you about his mother, yet. No, he didn't bring his mother on the date with him, but he might as well have. Forget about cutting the apron strings, the man still has his umbilical cord attached!

He kept getting calls and excusing himself from the table. Of course every time he came back we all got a fresh wave of foot, but I figured, the man's a doctor; he's on call. Deal with it.

Until I finally caught on it was a woman he was talking to, when during one of the calls, he didn't leave the table. At first, I thought, it must be a girlfriend or a wife since they were discussing fabrics for curtains. Wasn't too happy right about that moment. But no, it was his mother. He even apologized then and explained that she lived with him, and she was trying to redecorate the living room and was asking his opinion on things... during our date. Right. It couldn't wait until after dinner? Red flags popping up all over themselves here.

Well, Mother was widowed early in his life, and he couldn't very well make her live on her own after taking such good care of him all those years, could he? Far be it from me to come between a man and his mother. I was totally willing to bow out, but I would like to comment that if the man had a wife, at least she'd toss his stinky shoes and make sure he changed his socks!

* * *

I have yet to delete anyone's comment, but you've got to stop looking at Trent as a possibility in the man department. We don't date! Wednesday nights with Trent are more like therapy for both of us than actual dates. We have to eat before church; we both love Chinese and need a dose of it regularly to load up on MSG for the week. It's a given that we'll meet and do it together. That reminds me, it's about time for another Chinese run. Trent and I haven't had it for a while.

I'll give you a two-for. A couple of nights ago I went out with another of my dad's acquaintances. Cracker Barrel and a tractor show. Do you need any more details? I didn't think so. I think there may be a generation gap here. Dad needs to make younger friends.

Moving on to the next date: the history professor. He's another lead I picked up from Martin, the basketball/computer guy. He was somewhat like Martin, only not as much fun, and I mean that seriously. He's very cerebral, kind of like going back in time to an era when they talked in stilted language with no contractions and looked over their glasses at people much of the time like we're barbarians.

You'll have to take my word for that last part, because I assume you don't have a time machine. Let me know right away if you do; I'll go back in time and skip last night's date with Craig and maybe rethink this whole blind date thing.

Just kidding. I've learned to loosen up since my first date with Will. Honestly, though, if I had that first one to do over, when he pulled out the service dog vest, I would have just said "hasta la vista."

So Craig did not bring a dog on our date, but he did bring his pet: history. He loves history, carries it around with him, brings it out, pets it, and shows it off. I can see why this man is not in a relationship, though, because he slapped me upside the head with his history knowledge, then basically ignored me the rest of the evening.

How? I'm glad you asked. I'm sure that you are fully versed in every major and minor battle of each world war, but when he brought up the Battle of the Bulge I was just clueless. First he called it the Ardennes Counteroffensive, which completely eluded me. When he switched to The Battle of the Bulge, at least I'd heard of that. I made a joke about how I was constantly fighting that one (a little joke my mother always makes) thinking he could commiserate since he has a little tummy himself. Not only was he not amused, but he practically upbraided me for making a joke when we'd lost quite a few men during that battle. Well, I didn't mean to be flippant about the war; I was kidding. I told him so, and he kind of rolled his eyes and didn't say much the rest of the evening.

Pouting men get ignored back by me, so not much more was said for the rest of the night except, "Shall we go?" and "goodbye" (not good night). Well, goodbye to you Craig, and good luck.

* * *

I was kidding about the MSG. Several of you commented on that and the sodium content of Asian food. Focus people! This is not a nutritional site. I don't know if there actually is MSG in the food. It's salty, okay? A little egg foo yung is not going to kill me.

Let's skip through the next three dates I had with one statement: They were basically fun, not my kind of guy, and we didn't have a second date.

On to Darrin. I thought we had a winner with Darrin. He's a Christian. He seems kind. He has one major thing, though, and it's kind of debilitating - motion sickness. Let me give you an out right now if reading about gross things affects you in any way: skip this post.

So how many people would arrange a boat ride when they have motion sickness? I've got to hand it to Darrin for even attempting it; he's brave. He'd never been on a boat because he has gets so sick in cars, trains, and buses (maybe bikes, too, and pushing shopping carts for all I know) that he can't travel. Planes make his ears hurt. I know; he sounds kind of wimpy, but I don't think he can help it, so it's not fair to blame him.

Anyway, he got a kind of Dramamine that is non-drowsy, and he wanted to road test it in an actual sickness-inducing situation. So he got us tickets for a boat ride on the river. Sounds kind of calm doesn't it? It's not like it was the ocean. I would have chosen to use a patch myself, if I had motion sickness, but he was sure it wouldn't work. I think he was also a little sickened by the thought of absorbing something through his skin.

We met at the dock. I'm not sure why. In hindsight I wonder if it is because he could get somewhat sick even while driving himself across town. He was the only person alone on the dock, so I pegged him and introduced myself. Darrin is a pleasant man, kind of a regular-looking guy with a tasteful beard that he might want to rethink after today.

His motion sickness dominates not only his whole conversation, but his whole life, I gather. He's trying to go through some kind of training to overcome it, but it sounds like all it does is make him sick. I'm afraid this boat ride was part of his therapy. I don't mind helping a guy out if I can, but therapy isn't working. He started out by vomiting.

I shouldn't be that disgusted by it; after all he threw up in the river, I just have a thing about bodily fluids. I don't want to see them, and of course I don't want to smell them. Maybe it was just my imagination, but I could smell it on him the rest of the day. I tried to give him a piece of gum, but he just waved me off. He gave in and took his Dramamine as soon after his stomach settled as he could, but he looked kind of grey.

Well, guess what. He grabbed the wrong bottle. Now if he'd realized it, I bet he could have taken one tablet or half a tablet, but I saw him pop two Dramamine. As soon as he swallowed them, he realized his mistake, but it was too late.

The Dramamine hit him soon and hit him hard. He spent the whole trip with his head on my shoulder, drooling. Drool is not as bad as vomit, but it is still a bodily fluid and disgusting.

Now don't post comments on how cute your baby is even though he or she drools. I've got nieces and nephews, and I can take a little baby spit. This was man-sized drool along with breath that still smelled of vomit and his spit was caught up in his beard, so it didn't even evaporate.

Remember, you were warned.

He didn't wake up when the ship returned to the dock. What was I supposed to do with a drugged man? Bring him back to our house and let him sleep it off or try to get him to his place were my two options. I had a hard time trying to decide to do the right thing. I spent a little too much time talking myself out of the thought that his own bed was the place for him. I think it was all that drool that kept me from making up my mind right away. It did seem a little heartless to drag him back to his apartment (or wherever) and drop him on his doorstep. The river boat captain, or whatever they're called, helped me get him to my car and he napped on my back seat with his head on a beach towel I dug out of my trunk (sorry Darrin).

Grace was home, fortunately, and helped me get him to the couch. Before I could get him situated, he baptized the couch pillow with a good splotch of drool which disgusted Grace completely. (It's a family trait.)

A couple of hours later, he awoke, embarrassed to no end. I'm sure the awkwardness will keep him from ever calling me. I know the thought of the drool has decided it for me... never again. I drove him to his car at the dock, and we parted friends or rather distant acquaintances, because in spite of the fact that this man spent much of today drooling on my shoulder or sacked out on my couch, I barely spoke with him.

We promptly tossed the couch pillow.

Chapter Fourteen

Crazycatlady has posted the suggestion that my experiment isn't working. We've barely begun, people. My many siblings have several choices each for blind dates. Even my parents and friends have gotten into the spirit of this and set me up on dates. Well, Trent hasn't, but he said he'd try to think of someone for me. Nadine from work knew someone. Remember a couple of posts ago how I said that blind dates could be dangerous? It happened again.

I dropped in to see Nadine right before it was time to leave for the day. She sprang something on me.

"So I set you up with Geoffrey..." she said as soon as I entered her office. When someone starts a sentence like that it usually is continuing where you broke off in the middle of a conversation. I was totally blind-sided.

"Who?"

"My friend, Geoffrey. Remember I said I'd always thought you two would hit it off, but I didn't know until recently that you were cool with blind dates? I set it up like I said I would."

Does Nadine realize we had this conversation weeks ago? And all she did at the time was mention she had a friend. I didn't agree to go out with him. But I'm determined not to be a Grinch, to be open-minded, and just have fun, so I didn't fight it.

"Okay, which night is he free?"

"He has something else lined up instead of a standard date night."

"Like what?" I tried not to look suspicious, but remember I don't know the guy at all, and I only work with Nadine. Other than the gym episode, we haven't done anything together outside of work.

"Okay, now I want you to stay open-minded..."

Normally when someone says this to me, I instantly have red flags popping out all over the place, but since I'd just told myself this, I couldn't very well fault her for saying it.

"I'm open; I'm open. What does he want to do?"

"I think he's into fresh air and exercise."

"Okay," she was taking way too long to tell this.

"Plus, it's a good idea to be out in public for a date with someone you don't know."

I agreed with that one. This must have given her some confidence. She finally lowered the boom.

"Paintball." She smiled when she said it, but I could see she looked uncertain.

"Paintball?" Was she kidding?

She handed me a piece of paper with the name of the place written on it. She wasn't kidding.

"Just think about it," she said.

I'll be honest. I was stunned. When I envisioned blind dates I thought quiet dinners, movies, maybe a concert or even a picnic. I did not consider having people blast paint at me. I don't think that technically counts as a date.

I pretty much just left at that point. I didn't know what else to say to Nadine.

I went back to my office, closed my door, and looked up the paintball site from the paper. Should I be worried that it's on a street called Karnage? Yeah, like spelling carnage with a "k" makes it cute or something. This place boasted it was great for team-building and church groups. Really? Church groups? If I was to believe this site, if all of the employees at my non-profit head out to Karnage Road and shoot each other with paint pellets we're going to work better together? I don't see the connection.

Then it occurred to me the idea might be to band together and shoot other companies or organizations. Everyone knows it's team building to obliterate, say the Girl Scouts or Goodwill.

We wouldn't be doing the group version, though. This could be cathartic, I guess, in a violent sort of way. Anyway, Nadine had already set up the "date" for me.

I know you're probably thinking that maybe Nadine does not have my best interests in mind. She's the one who gave me the aloe vera that I was allergic to. She talked me into tagging along with her at the gym while she flirted with the personal trainer. She also got me to think of the lunch meeting I had with Jack as a date. Now everything is awkward with him, even an innocent bouquet of flowers. I looked at the paper with the information on it. It didn't say the day.

I picked up the phone and dialed her extension. "This paper says 11 o'clock. What day is this event?"

There was a pause. I looked at the phone to see if we were still connected.

"Hello?"

"Tomorrow," she said. Then she hung up the phone. She wasn't getting off that easily. I headed straight for her office. She'd grabbed her purse and was almost out the door.

"Tomorrow?" I said. "What if I'm busy?"

"You'd cancel," she said sweetly.

"Cancel the date, you mean," I muttered on my way back to my

138

office.

"I heard that," she called after me like by that point I cared.

I wasn't busy, and I didn't cancel, but I seriously thought about it. A lot of girls said online that they love paintball. I stayed up half the night researching paintball and planning my outfit. I mean a girl's got to look good while she's being pelted with paint, right? I thought it would be cute to wear polka dots, but I didn't want to give anyone a target. Too bad, too, because I have this top that is multiple colored giant dots that would have been perfect.

My plan, though, is basically the same as when I go skiing. It consists of staying in the lodge and switching between drinking hot cocoa with whipped cream and yummy lattes. This paintball place will surely have its version of a ski lodge, and when Geoff is done artistically blowing people up with paintball grenades, he can join me in the paint lodge for a mocha.

But as we all know, the best laid plans o' mice and men...

* * *

I rolled out of bed at 10:00, got dressed, and headed for the paint place. I stopped at Starbucks on the way in case I was wrong about the paint lodge having good coffee, and arrived a few minutes before eleven.

I sipped my coffee, studying the place. It was swarming with guys. How would I find him?

I didn't need to worry. When I checked in, he found me. Not hard to figure out, since I was the only unattached woman there. Geoff seemed nice enough, clear blue eyes, cute blond hair, kind of curly like he was on the verge of needing a haircut. He had one errant curl that just needed tucking. Before I knew it my hand was reaching for it...

Yes, I did. Before we even introduced ourselves I was about to fix his hair! What am I, his mom? It was incredibly embarrassing, but honestly my hand just moved on its own. I swear I've never done anything like that before. Okay, maybe something like it, but not lately.

He didn't seem to notice. At least he didn't say anything about it, just introduced himself. He got me set up with my gear, including goggles, gun, and ammo. Never thought I'd ever need ammunition for a date.

Now in case you've never done this before, I'll describe it for you. It's a barbaric and messy form of capture the flag where people you don't even know want you dead. A game lasts until everyone is shot up with paint pellets. The Web site said it feels like the snap of a rubber band to be shot with a pellet. I can only surmise that the person who wrote that either has never been snapped with a rubber band or used a giant rubber band for the trial run. A warning about wearing padding would have been helpful.

Now, remember I am trying not to be a drag about these dates, but this almost became my last one. It hurt! It hurt a lot! After the first round I would have sat out the rest of the rounds in the paint lodge, but it was more like a paint shack. They served substandard coffee that wasn't even hot and powdered creamer. In case you don't know the ins and outs of powdered creamer, it won't dissolve in lukewarm coffee, and you end up stirring a lump of it around and around and around. So, instead of relaxing in the "lodge," I hid in the bushes as far away from all of the lunatics as I could get.

Great plan, right? Wrong! Someone (I suspect it was Geoff) must have thought that was cheating, because someone kept firing round after round at my hiding place! He even went so far as to explode a paint grenade over me! When the whole thing was over, the date was over. What were we supposed to do; go out to eat splattered with paint and mud?

Did I forget to mention the mud? Yeah, I ungracefully slid face first in the mud trying to escape from some punk kid who singled me out at the beginning, gleefully chasing me down. Perhaps if Geoff had come to my rescue instead of laughing at my dilemma I would have escaped the mud at least.

He must have had fun. He talked about going on another date, but I graciously declined saying that it seemed that we just didn't enjoy the same pastimes. He was nice about it.

Worry not. There's always someone else waiting in the wings. I already have another date lined up, and this one is a blast from the past. But that is another blog.

Chapter Fifteen

It sounded like a lot of you enjoyed hearing about my paintball
ordeal. Some of you even plan to try it yourself. I'm guessing those were
guys. Odd, because I figured all of my readers were women. Well, have
fun. Isn't that a perfectly good waste of paint? Just putting that out there.

When I got back to my car, I had two messages on my cell. (I left it
in there for its own protection. If only I had been so kind to myself.) One
was from my sister, Ruth. She sounded a little perturbed about how my
date went with Tyler. (a.k.a.: What IS his name?) I think she had visions
of me with the cute little Italian kiddos too, because she was very
disappointed... but in me! She had some money from Tyler to pay for the
date. Whatever. I deleted her message.

The other one was from my sister Lydia. I haven't mentioned
Lydia yet, have I? She's two years older than I am, a kind soul, very
sympathetic. She's the type who's never met a stranger, because as soon
as they meet her, and they sense that she's so sensitive, they pour out their
woes to her. Well, it turns out she'd run into Ben at some function or
other. Ben was my old boyfriend from college. He was a little on the large
size, like a big overstuffed teddy bear. Well, maybe you couldn't actually

call him a boyfriend. We went out a few times, but we didn't date for very long because he switched schools and moved to California. Keeping up the long distance relationship didn't work for us.

Well, old Ben had moved back to town and hadn't made a lot of friends yet, so Lydia decided it would be nice to get him involved in the community (read: date me). But seriously, she's planned this fun double date with her husband, Ken, and Ben and me for tonight. I don't know if you can call this a blind date, because I already knew him, but either way we're going to dinner and a movie.

I remember Ben being fun and very sweet. I think he liked to give presents. I don't have anything he gave me, though. In fact, I don't remember what the gifts were. A teddy bear maybe?

I'll check back after the date is over. I have a lot to do to get ready. Just scraping off the mud will take a while. I've also got to get this paint out of my clothes. I was promised it would come out easily. We'll see. And after crawling around in the bushes for hours, I'm bushed. I need a nap.

* * *

I have several welts from my paintball date! A word to the wise is sufficient: for women, anyway, find something else to do with your Saturday if you're ever invited to go. Any men out there, knock yourselves out.

Meanwhile... back to my dating life. I have mixed feelings about tonight. Some good things happened, some not so good, and some surprises thrown in just to keep the continuing downward spiral of a deep vortex that is my dating life going at full speed.

We all met at Lydia's house. Ben arrived with a small bouquet of flowers, which I put in water. I just remembered I forgot and left them over there. Too bad, it was so sweet of him to do that. He looked just like I remembered him; maybe his blond hair is a little lighter. He's been living in California, so I guess the sun bleached it. He still reminds me of a big, stuffed bear.

After a nice dinner at El Chico's (Lydia's favorite restaurant) we all drove together to the movie that will forever after be known as "That Loser Movie." It stank big time. Ben and Ken were supposed to pick a light-hearted feel-good romance that we could all enjoy. Lydia and I take no blame for their poor selection or for leaving halfway through it. Second, when it started to go south fast and Ken, Lydia, and I decided we'd had enough of it, and we were out of there, where do you think Ben was? Mr. I Have To See The End No Matter How Disgusting was bolted to his seat. So the three of us went to the coffee shop across the street from the theater complex to wait. We spent an enjoyable hour drinking lattes and eating rich desserts that none of us had any business eating. Well, me, anyway, until I lose a few pounds.

When Ben rolled out of the theater with the six other people who made it through That Loser Movie to the end, he joined us. He then proceeded to tell us what happened in it, even though we made it clear we didn't want to know.

Okay, now you will all agree with me at the outset that the next thing is pretty out there. Guess who walked in. I'm tempted to stop right here, and not tell you and let you all post your guesses, but we can do it honor system. Post it below before you keep reading.

Some of you will probably guess. It was Geoff, the paintball guy! I guess young, good-looking guys will always end up at coffee shops when you're there with another good-looking guy. I think it's like a law of the universe. Either that or he often goes there, but I'd never noticed him before because I hadn't met him yet.

I was determined not to be embarrassed. You can do it, you know, if you convince yourself that it's no big deal. Geoff and I hadn't really hit it off, but we'd parted amicably, so I waved him over and introduced him to my sister and to Ken. When we got to Ben, I introduced him as an old friend from college. Well, it was true, wasn't it? And what was I supposed to say, "You were my blind date this morning; this is my blind date for tonight"?

Geoff and his friend, I forgot his name, joined us, and I thought we all got along amazingly well considering most of us didn't know each other before the day began. We had a lot in common including, but not limited to a general agreement that life was so much better with good chocolate. We all ordered more desserts and more coffee. I went for decaf for this one.

After about an hour, Geoff and his friend left, and Lydia, Ken, and I were ready to go, too. I think Ben would have sat there all night, sipping strong coffee and discussing current movies. He must be a night owl, because we were yawning all over the place, but he suggested we see a late show. I guess he's one of those big movie buffs who have to see everything that comes out. I casually mentioned that we had to get up for church to see if that was part of his life, and Ben said he hadn't found a church yet after moving back. Lydia suggested he come to ours. So tomorrow Ben is joining us. I do not consider that a date, but it's good to know he shares my faith. Obviously, that's a deal breaker.

I didn't get a chance to talk to Ben alone much, but maybe tomorrow I'll get to know him better. This is the only blind date that led to a second date, assuming we go out for lunch after church like Grace and I usually do.

Good night, I'll let you know what happens tomorrow.

* * *

Many of you voted for Geoff as the one who showed up. Very good guess! Several posted you thought it was amazing that we ended up at the same place (laws of the universe not withstanding). Some of you thought he was stalking me. Geoff is the antithesis of a stalker. Totally sweet and as much not the stalker type as a guy could be. We might have hit it off if he didn't enjoy violent games so much.

Anyway, fast forward to today and Ben joining us at church. He got lost and couldn't find the church until the service was almost over, but he did join Grace and me for lunch afterward. Too bad he missed the service. The sermon was on dating, marriage, and being the right person rather than only looking for the right person. It was right in line with what's been happening in my life.

After church we decided to meet at Panera, which was packed, but we still managed to get a table together in the back. While we were sitting there, Tyler came in. Remember the guy who forgot his wallet? I did not invite him over. He pretended not to see me. Oh, he saw me all right. He kept moving to the big table next to us in the corner to sit with the group he was with, but I saw him kind of hesitate at first, like he was saying to himself "How do I know her? Oh no, she's that nightmare date!"

Forget what I said about how you can be determined not to be embarrassed. It has to work both ways. If someone studiously avoids looking at you, it's not comfortable. Especially since we'd just sat down, so we were there for another forty-five minutes. He was practically sitting next to me. Oh the laws of the universe were against me for sure.

After lunch, Ben wanted to go see another movie, but since I was at paintball yesterday and then took a long nap, I had some things to catch up on like laundry and errands. Ben seemed disappointed. He's so sweet; I felt bad about saying "no thanks," but I was sore from paintball, too, and needed some down time to take a nap and putz around. We arranged to go out Monday night. There is another movie he wants to see. I'm guessing there is always another movie he wants to see.

I can't say that I know too much more about Ben than I did last night. I barely remember him from college. I'm looking forward to going out just the two of us.

That reminds me, Trent and I haven't gone for Chinese in a very long time. I've been so busy, I haven't had time.

Meanwhile, I feel a nap coming on.

Chapter Sixteen

I got to work this morning bright and early, but not earlier than Zoe. She's always the first one here. When I walked into my office there was a large box of candy on my desk. There was no note on it. I assumed it was from Jack, but how could it be? He wasn't there yet. Zoe came into my office to update me about a meeting. I wondered if I should ask her where the candy came from. I didn't want to bring up the whole Jack thing. I didn't need to decide. She brought it up.

"Is the candy from your 'secret admirer' too?" she said. I think I turned red at that one.

"I don't know. I was wondering where it came from."

She looked like she didn't believe me. I've worked here for years and never had so much as a miniature Snickers appear. Not until Jack started, so maybe I don't blame her.

"A guy dropped it off right before you got here."

"A delivery man?" Is there such a thing as a candy delivery man?

"I don't know, some blond guy." I think she was getting a little bored with the conversation, because she handed me the agenda for a meeting and left.

Well, no use letting good candy go to waste. And it was good candy, too. I had a nut cluster. It was so good; I had the other one. Nadine came into my office while I was munching on the second nut cluster. No doubt it was to see what happened Saturday, but when she saw the giant box of candy, she said, "May I?" and helped herself to a piece at my nod. Obviously, Annika can't eat such a large box by herself. She studied the diagram included in the lid before helping herself to another piece.

"So how did it go with Geoffrey?"

Why does she keep calling him that? He called himself Geoff. How would I describe him and the date to her? Juicy? Is she waiting to hear that I think he's juicy?

"Violent," was what I decided on.

She dropped the box of candy. Nadine tends toward the dramatic. Fortunately, the box landed on my desk. All that happened was a few pieces popped out. I jiggled the box until they went back into place, put the lid on, and put in on the credenza for safekeeping. The roses were wilted. I threw them in the wastebasket.

"You didn't like him?" She said it like the thought never occurred to her.

"We just didn't hit it off. I'm not into shooting or paint or running around on a Saturday afternoon shooting paint."

"Well, I'm sure that's not all he likes to do," she said.

"He likes coffee and dessert," I said and told her about running into him at the coffee shop.

"You're meant for each other. It's fate." Funny how people who don't believe in God will believe in a mysterious, fickle thing called fate to govern their lives.

"It was chance; like when I ran into Tyler at Panera's." I told her about what happened Sunday. "Are we meant for each other, too?"

Oh no, she didn't think so. Sorry Nadine, you can't have it both ways. Maybe it was just an opportunity for us to make things right, and I definitely felt good about how everything turned out with both guys. I'm not meant to be with someone who won't even acknowledge my existence a few days after spending an evening with me. And I'm not meant to be with a guy who thinks it's fun to explode paint grenades over my head.

"I'm still not giving up on Geoffrey," she said.

I wanted to say "Then you date him - wear padding," but I changed the subject instead. "How's Tom?"

She didn't answer, just looked around for the box of candy.

"You know, Tom, the juicy fitness guy you scooped up at the fitness center."

She was moving toward the candy again and ignoring me, so I let it drop. It takes a lot of nerve to go after a girl's chocolate when she's put it out of your reach. I had a meeting with Jack in a few minutes anyway, which I told her about so she would get along to her own office before she downed half the box.

I also thought that might jog her memory and make her want to talk about Jack, and how I was doing with him, but at least she took the hint about the candy and left.

When I got to Jack's office, the door was partway open, so I knocked lightly and walked in. He was standing in front of the mirror again, adjusting his tie, smoothing his hair, seeing if his suit coat was wrinkled in the back. The guy does an inordinate amount of primping in my opinion. I mean, isn't that one of the good things about being a guy? They don't have to fuss with their appearance to look good. I hadn't realized he was so into his looks.

Jack started a little when he saw me, then smoothly took control of the situation, having me sit down, asking if I wanted something to drink.

When no one else showed up, I asked Jack who else was included in the meeting. He said Nadine was coming to talk about an event that was on the horizon. Funny that she didn't say she was coming to the meeting too, when I mentioned it.

She showed up a couple of minutes later. I saw her exchange a smile with Jack before she sat down next to me. Was she going to try to steal him now, too?

As soon as she opened her mouth, I could see she had a huge chunk of chocolate in her teeth. I have to say that I felt a little tinge of satisfaction. I was immediately ashamed for feeling that way, so I gestured to her about her teeth. I am nothing if not loyal... eventually.

She excused herself and came back with white teeth, smelling minty fresh.

Later after the meeting was over, and Nadine had left, Jack put away a folder, then rose and closed the door to his office. I wondered if I was in trouble for something.

He asked me out again! Or rather we're having another lunch meeting. He has some ideas he wants to try out on me, he said, before he presents them to the board. We're going out for lunch today. I'm not telling Nadine this time, since she didn't seem very interested in how the last meeting went.

I'll let you know how my lunch date goes... yes "date."

* * *

I got a lot of agreement about Nadine and the chocolate. I couldn't believe she was so aggressive. When I got back from lunch, it looked like more was gone. For goodness sake, does a girl have to lock up her chocolate?

Some of you continued along the vein that I shouldn't be dating my boss. Wait until you've read this post. You may feel a little better about the whole thing.

This wasn't the best lunch meeting I've ever had. It started out well, but by the time it was over, I decided I'd have to change my name and have plastic surgery so no one would recognize me at Fujiyama's. Either that or find another place for takeout.

Jack felt like Japanese for lunch today. That's fine with me; I like Asian food. I like Fujiyama's. But no, he said we should have sushi. More power to him. I don't eat raw fish. He talked me into promising to try some of the rolls that didn't have raw fish in them. My favorite was one with spicy crab on top, so I thank him for introducing me to an interesting new food I hadn't tried. That's all I'll thank him for.

When I walked into Fujiyama's I immediately felt at peace. I don't know if it was the man playing quiet, tasteful tunes on the piano in the corner, or the minimalist, traditional Asian decorations that put me at ease. I thought it was a wonderful place to take a relaxing break during a busy workday.

Jack had arrived before I did and had a head start on me on the sake. A huge head start and one that I would never catch up to considering I don't drink. When I told the waitress that I'd have tea, Jack interrupted. "No, bring Annika some suki!"

Yes, he did say that. I, of course, declined to have suki and went with tea.

Jack likes to eat well. He had a tasteful assortment of sushi rolls waiting on the table for us. He likes his sake, too, and when I say likes, I don't mean one cup. The more he drank the friendlier he got. Pretty soon he was cozied up next to me a little too close for a business meeting. He's a touchy feely kind of guy anyway, but this was basically draping himself and using me as the window.

Yes, that was embarrassing. Yes, I put a stop to all that togetherness. Just when I was trying to decide if I should leave, Jack decided for me. He started to sing.

Now I don't mean hum. You can pull that off in public if you do it quietly. Even whistling is socially acceptable in some situations. No, the man belted out a tune.

I think the guy doodling around on the piano might have been the owner's son. I'd barely noticed he was there, but Jack latched onto him. He sat down next to him on the piano bench, slung an arm across the guy's shoulder and started singing Billy Joel's "Piano Man"! I'm not sure why the guy decided to humor him, but Fujiyama's own "piano man" started to accompany him.

I had barely begun my lunch, but I decided I'd had enough. I stopped at the piano on my way out telling Jack that I had to get back to the office and left. I didn't even get a to-go box for the food. I was a little sad to say goodbye to the California roll.

I don't think Jack noticed I'd left. He'd reached the part about wearing "a younger man's clothes," and he was swaying with tears running down his cheeks! Honestly! He's not even that old!

I made a statement, leaving him like that, but now I'm hungry. So guess what the rest of my lunch consists of? Yep, chocolates.

And all of the nutrition police don't need to leave a comment below. I know I should have eaten my lunch. I can almost hear you saying "Candy is not a meal."

I have to say that a little rice, seaweed, and a tiny bit of meat is also probably not much of a meal, especially since I had time to eat only a couple of rolls. The idea of eating seaweed is a little off-putting. Am I the only person who sees the word "weed" in there? Since when did I start eating weeds?

I guess the same time I started having lunch dates with sake-imbibing bosses. Well, that's over. I would have thrown away his chocolates, except, well, I'm hungry, and they're good.

I'm okay with this lunch semi-dating ending. I mean Jack is good-looking and all, but I never did figure out where this was supposed to be going. A couple of lunch dates, and flowers and candy, but he didn't ever seem to actually be interested in me. He didn't stop by my office to talk to me or invite me on a real date. It's kind of a relief anyway, because I don't approve of dating your boss, conflict of interest and all that.

Jack had an appointment with a large donor at around 5:00. He rolled in a little before that. I saw him plop Alka-seltzer into a cup and drink some when I walked by his office a few minutes later. He swished it around and finished it off; then he leaned back in his chair. I paused. Should I get everything out in the open once and for all; let him know I'm just not interested in continuing this office romance?

He opened his eyes when I entered his office. He looked like he wanted to say something, but instead just closed his eyes again. It was time to let him know where we stand.

I closed the door. That roused him. He groaned a little as if the sight of me was making him sick and closed his eyes again. This man just can't hold his sake.

"Jack," I began and waited for his eyes to open. They didn't. I said his name again. He opened his eyes and burped. I slowly stepped back a pace or two to miss that. He sat up in his chair and raked his fingers through his hair.

"Yeah?" he sounded weary.

"Jack, while I appreciate the lunch invitations, the flowers, and the box of candy, I don't feel continuing this is in either of our best interests or the good of the company."

He looked at me slightly puzzled like I'd spoken in Russian, then nodded like the translation had just come delayed through an earpiece. He said "okay" and put his head down on his folded arms. Was he going to conduct a meeting in this condition? The donor would be arriving any minute.

I guess the same thought occurred to him, and he decided he had to get out of there. He stood and started for the door. Then he stopped. "Wait, box of candy?"

I nodded. "Even the candy."

At that moment Zoe knocked and ushered the donor in.

Jack recovered nicely, guiding the man to a chair, simultaneously slipping into his jacket, combing his fingers through his hair while giving it a glance in the mirror as he passed, and popping a breath mint. I moved on to my office. The guy sure was smooth.

And so my first and last office romance ends, and things will get back to normal. Obviously, romance does not belong in a place where business is conducted.

Chapter Seventeen

I know you will be suitably outraged when you hear what I learned today. Nadine has been dating Jack behind my back! I should have known. If a girl will go after your chocolate, she'll go after your man.

Okay, I know he's not exactly my man, but she's the one who wanted me to date him, and don't forget that she swooped down on Tom the fitness guy when he was supposed to be for me, too. Who's the one doing the dating experiment, after all?

And let me save you the trouble of pointing out that I pretty much dumped him, and that he's all wrong for me. Neither of those points matter when your friend steals your date. Make that ex-friend.

When I came in this morning, Zoe handed me my messages. I continued on to my office. I stopped just inside the door and was leafing through them when I came to one that was for Nadine... from Jack! It said something like, "Meet me at La Boheme at 8:00." Isn't that nice? He takes her out for a night on the town, while I get lunch and a box of chocolates. I looked up to see Zoe watching me. So it was no accident that I got Nadine's message. I don't know if Zoe was trying to help me or hurt me, but I'm glad she did what she did. I know now I did right to break things off.

So all of you who were down on Jack were right. That's okay. I have a date with Ben tonight. A real date at night. I don't know what we're doing yet. Maybe we'll go to La Boheme.

* * *

Thank you for the show of support regarding Nadine and Jack going out behind my back. I feel better knowing you're on my side. Mommyninjawarriorprincess commented that this is one of the reasons office dating should be off limits. I'm willing to concede it wasn't the best idea I've had.

Ben and I did not go to La Boheme; we went to a movie. When Ben picked me up, I casually mentioned La Boheme was playing. It's not that I exactly wanted to go, I just wanted to see how flexible Ben is. He wasn't interested at all.

I may have overreacted a bit yesterday, calling Nadine my ex-friend. I just wish she'd talked to me about it rather than hide it. She did, after all, break the code.

But back to Ben. He wanted to eat at Fuddruckers before the movie. I'd never been there. I'm not that in to hamburgers. They're okay sometimes. Ben mentioned how he loves Fuddruckers when we went out for Mexican the other night. At least he didn't order the giant burger. I got some onion rings that were awesome, so it wasn't a complete loss. And it seemed to me a milkshake was just about necessary. If I'm forced to eat a hamburger, it's only right I get a giant chocolate milkshake to wash it down.

It was noisy, though. They could have used some noise-absorbing materials, like carpet, instead of wooden floors. We could hear tons of video games going off the whole time. I hate that. Also they kept calling out people's names for their orders. All that noise at any time would be annoying, but especially when I'm trying to get to know someone. I couldn't wait to get out of there. Ben didn't seem to even notice the noise.

I like to try new places, quiet places. I usually try things like Lebanese or Italian, something interesting. Even at Mexican places where I've eaten before, I can try cuisine I haven't had. Ben seemed to enjoy his hamburger, though.

I can't say I liked the movie as much as he did, either. I tried to stay as long as I could, but I feel plot is everything. I can stand a little violence and gore if there is a plot. But I don't need to be horrified just for the sake of it. And would it kill the writer to give us a little dialog? I left and went to the coffee shop across the street again.

Someone I used to go to college with came in and ended up joining me. Brent, or is it Brett? Something like that. I think he's interested in Grace. He kept asking things about her, like what she's doing. Is she married, etc. He's not right for her. He comes off as kind of immature for his age. He's a nice guy, just seems like he never grew up.

Ben joined us after about 15 minutes. He and Brent/Brett shook hands, and Ben got a giant coffee smoothie thing with whipped cream that I normally would have been coveting if I hadn't already filled up to the brim on chocolate shake with whipped cream and a cherry on top. Did I mention that at Fuddruckers they bring out the giant metal mixing cup with the rest of the shake in there? So, it's almost like two milkshakes. I was drinking a simple latte, decaf, to finish off the night. I can't sleep in, in the morning, since I'm a working girl.

At the first yawn from my mouth, Ben suggested we get going, so he took me home kind of early. He was quiet in the car, so maybe he was tired too, or jealous of Brent/Brett. Usually he's all Mr. Chatty about the movie. I didn't miss the play by play a bit. We're slated to go out again tomorrow. I'll let you know what's happening. I'll tell you right now, I'm not getting to know him as quickly as you might think. Between the noisy restaurant, the movie, and the quick end to the date, there just wasn't a lot of sharing going on.

* * *

Ben and I went to Red Robin last night for supper. Next time, Annika needs to pick the restaurant. I cannot eat hamburgers every time we go out.

Annika needs to pick the movie next time, too, since it looks like that's all we're going to do, watch movies... violent ones. I mean I understand that guys like that sort of thing, but is a steady diet of violence good for anybody? I'll tell you, I'm getting tired of walking out of movies. You'd think Ben would tire of paying full price for me to walk out. Wouldn't he consult me before he picks the show anyway? We're both on the date here, Ben. Maybe he thinks that since he's paying, that I'm fine with him choosing. Actually, I don't know what he's thinking. He's not a big sharer of what's going on in his head. A little consideration goes a long way; especially since he doesn't have any idea what I like. I thought that was what dating was supposed to be about, getting to know each other.

So I sat there in the coffee shop for a full hour. My phone needed charging, but I didn't have a charger with me, so I was afraid of running down the battery by passing the time calling someone or texting. I just sat there sipping my decaf latte and staring out the window. Should a girl have to bring what, a book on her date? Provide her own entertainment? Because this was all wrong.

Ben eventually joined me and ordered his giant fluffy drink again. I stuck with my decaf. It was getting pretty late by that time. I was yawning, but Ben didn't suggest we go this time. Maybe he didn't care for Brent last night, and wanted to leave just to get away from him. He went to great lengths to discuss movie plot while we sat there, like I cared if some action hero saved the world from being blown to smithereens... again.

As an experiment, I started fake yawning, a lot. We still sat there. Eventually, I suggested we might want to get going because we had to get up for work the next day. He seemed to be reluctant to leave even then. When he pulled up in front of my house I thanked him and escaped.

Yes, escaped.

* * *

Tonight I had my last date with Ben. Eating only hamburgers and seeing violent movies was getting on my nerves, yes, but there was another problem seething beneath the surface that I didn't even know

167

about.

So we went to Fuddrucker's again. Ben must be a regular at this place. I skipped the burger and just got onion rings and the chocolate shake. A girl can burn off only so many calories sitting behind a desk all day, so I figured I might as well get the good stuff. Ben looked at me like I was from another planet when I explained that I was tired of eating hamburgers. I ignored the look.

I know there was no nutritional value in this meal, but I ate a good lunch. Besides we broke up, so I don't have to worry about my future stretching out in a long line of hamburger joints anymore.

So after "dinner" I asked (rather cheerily I thought) what we were going to do now. I got the "What do you think we're going to do, you alien, you?" look again from Ben, which I ignored again.

He named a movie. I suggested a different one. He said he wasn't interested in the one I picked. I said I wasn't interested in his choice. So we went to a different one that neither of us particularly wanted to see. I was actually making it almost to the end of this one until several scenes in a row came up that were particularly bad. I left, determined that it would be the last evening I spent by myself in a coffee shop. But I waited alone for only a few minutes before someone came in. It was Geoff again - paintball guy! He was just stopping for a coffee, but when he saw me, and heard my story, he sat down to keep me company until Ben showed.

May I say that Geoff has improved a lot since that first date, or at least my opinion of him has improved. Of course he looked good the first time I met him, but no one looks good covered with mud and paint, so that great first impression was quickly replaced with a reality check, especially since he was so aggressive with the paint.

It was only ten minutes before Ben came out of the movie. He didn't look happy. He plunked himself down in a chair without even getting coffee. Great, now he was Mr. Pouty. Yeah, I don't play games with grown men who act like children, so I suggested we go. Ben gave me a look I couldn't place, maybe resentful, distrustful even. Geoff must have noticed the grim look because he offered to give me a ride home.

That's when Mr. Pouty morphed into Mr. Hyde. He jumped up so fast his chair fell over backward. I thought he was going to punch Geoff. I wouldn't say that Geoff was aggressive, but he certainly didn't back down. Just the opposite, he took a step forward which placed him between Ben and me. I assured Geoff I would be fine, and Ben and I left.

I don't get men. None of these guys seem to really be interested in me, yet when push comes to shove (almost literally) they're ready to fight. It's probably just their egos.

Not that I don't have ego problems, but I'm on record against brawling in coffee shops.

* * *

I didn't finish my story.

So on the way home, I'm busy letting Ben down easily, and he's busy driving or listening to the radio or I don't know, lost in thought? Maybe he was still seething about his near altercation with Geoff. Anyway, he must have tuned me out because when we reached my house, I had to say it all over again.

Yeah, he doesn't let down easily, this one. In fact, he explodes. So, pouting, exploding, I figure I'm dodging a bullet with him. After calling me ungrateful when it comes to gifts, (I guess he found out I left his flowers at Lydia's house.) he insisted he still wanted to date. Well, sorry to be so blunt, Ben old buddy, but it doesn't work that way. Especially after throwing the flowers in my face (not literally). I didn't mean to leave them over there, after all.

It came down to I couldn't convince him of anything. And that's how we parted.

I can't help but feel like there should have been something I could have said to make him understand that we don't have anything in common. I'm sure the reason we couldn't keep up the long distance relationship when he moved away for college was because we just don't care about each other that way. At least I don't, and I don't see that he was so enamored with me.

When I told Grace about all of it, she thought he was probably jealous of Geoff and Brent/Brett. After all, I did end up sitting there in the coffee shop with Brett/Brent once and Geoff twice. Maybe he thinks I'm a flirt. I'm not; I didn't invite those guys. I ran into them accidentally. Fortunately, I don't care what Ben thinks. That ship has sailed, our relation-ship. On to the next blind date.

Chapter Eighteen

A lot of you were glad I said arrivederci to Ben, since you didn't think he was right for me from the start. One of you called him an inconsiderate dolt, selfish to the core. Well, I'm not disagreeing, but probably best if we don't start name calling. Especially after what I did tonight.

I did something I'm not proud of. In fact, I'm plainly ashamed. Confession is good for the soul, so I'll share it with all of you. My brother, Paul, set me up with a blind date for tonight. My phone wasn't charged, so all I heard was that he set me up with Ed, and the date was at 6:00. Fine, I deal with ambiguity better than I used to after all that has happened to me this month. Edward and I would have a grand old time.

Well, someone unplugged the charger from the wall. Grace swears she didn't touch it, and I know I didn't, but the thing was not charged, so I turned my phone off so it would charge faster. When I discovered it, I hadn't been able to check my phone, so I wore my standard outfit for dates when I don't know where I'm going: nice slacks, a nice blouse and light jacket. Well, 6:00 came and went, and no Edward showed up. I finally remembered my dead/charging phone, and checked it, and Paul had arranged for me to meet Ed at the restaurant. Only, now his name was Eddie, the restaurant was Longhorn Steakhouse, and I was told to dress casually.

Panic mode struck. No time to change clothes, and I didn't have Eddie's phone number, so I called Paul, who didn't answer. I jumped in the car and headed for Longhorn while trying to message Paul. Just as I arrived, a man came out of the restaurant looking miffed, and I knew it had to be Eddie. He had on western wear, boots, even a cowboy hat, and walked with a purpose toward a large truck. I could have just gotten quietly back in my car and left, but I'm not the kind of person who blows people off, so I ran over to the man I was sure was Eddie and introduced myself. Well, he calmed down when he heard my dead phone story, and helped me into his truck, which was quite a leap up, and we were off. I didn't know where we were off to, but we were off.

So I don't know if Eddie got a chance to eat, I assume so, but he didn't ask if I'd eaten. We talked about the usual things you talk about on a first date, where you work, what you do, on the way there. He's a real estate broker.

Next thing I knew we were pulling into the speedway. I've never been to the speedway, never had any desire to go, because all they do there is race things, which I truly hate. Please don't write to me and tell me how you love racing and racetracks, trying to convince me that it's the most fun you've ever had. From what I've seen on TV, it's an endless, monotonous circle of cars going around and around broken up by people crashing. So, boring and horrifying both. What's not to love? Well, all of it, so I never go.

I'm not saying there is anything morally wrong with racing. I just don't like it. Well, Eddie was under the impression that I'd been told what the date tonight was, and I had been, theoretically, except for my stupid phone, so what was I supposed to do? Make him leave? He was obviously thrilled to be there. So I steeled myself for another boring and perhaps horrifying evening, where I was going to sit and starve.

I didn't have to starve; there was a concession stand with the standard hot dog again or burger that tasted like it was fried on someone's manifold. No thanks. Well, it certainly wasn't Eddie's fault. Longhorn is a nice place. I sat there in the stands waiting for it to begin thinking about the thick, juicy steak I could have had if my stupid phone hadn't let me down. I would have had the loaded baked potato with cheese and bacon bits. Real ones, not those awful fake soy things.

It was pretty noisy already, so Eddie couldn't hear my stomach growling, but I could feel it, and I was feeling pretty sorry for myself. The stands weren't the cleanest spot in the world, either, and boy did I look out of place. Have you ever tried to walk on bleachers in heels? It doesn't work very well. Eddie tried to help me, but there's only so much you can do to help someone walk in spike heels up rows and rows of bleachers.

So the event starts, and low and behold, it's not a car race, it's a show. I'm almost relieved for a brief moment until I realize it's a monster truck show. A huge truck drove into the arena and everyone stood up and clapped. And I'm so out of it, that I clapped too until I realize the truck can't hear me, and I don't know the driver.

I could have lasted the night if I'd had some food, but I just couldn't hack it on the three stale peppermints I found in the bottom of my purse. And that's when it hits me. My phone is still almost dead, so I can't use it for entertainment. It's too noisy to even talk to Eddie, and my car is parked at Longhorn. So when we leave, I could just get something to go from Longhorn. I sigh in relief, wondering how long this thing could last. Well, I picked up a program someone dropped, and realized nothing would be open except Taco Bell by the time this monster event was over.

Here's the part I'm not proud of: before I could talk myself out of it, I made my alarm go off on my phone. It sounds like a ringer. And then I pretended there was some kind of emergency that I was needed for, and I ran out of there. Eddie tried to go with me, but I told him I was fine. I didn't want to spoil his evening any more than I had. I'd already made him eat alone, made him almost late, made him pay for my ticket and wasted it, and made him attend his truck thing alone. Yeah, I wasn't too proud of myself.

I called a cab, went to Longhorn and got something to go. Grace was gone when I got home, so I ate in front of the TV watching something I'd recorded. A commercial came on for the monster truck show. I should have felt relieved that I hadn't just spent an entire evening there, but I just felt guilt. If I hadn't run out on Eddie, I would have been willing to try going out again, but that won't be happening.

It's just occurred to me that as I have bared my anonymous heart to you day by day that, in a way, you know me better than the people who know mostly the outward me. That Annika doesn't say everything she's thinking, of course. Strange thought... you know me so well, yet you don't know me at all. If you saw me walking down the street, you'd walk right on by.

* * *

I thought we were having an adventure here together, people. A lot of you were very blunt about my less than stellar behavior last night. In a way I don't blame you. I freely confessed I was wrong. In fact, I would've bet money that I'd never do something like that, except I don't bet. You do realize I could have just skipped posting that date, right? No one would've been the wiser. I'm baring my soul for you people. While I appreciate your honesty, just remember to keep it kind.

As for Annikawhatareyouthinking, you are way too harsh. I can block people on here, you know.

"To err is human..." so let's just forgive Annika and forget that date ever happened. I am.

Ben has left me several voicemail messages and texted me that he wants to get back together. I am ignoring them and him. I don't know how much clearer I can be that I'm not interested in him.

One of you commented that I haven't been out with Trent lately. I just have been busy, so unfortunately I haven't had time to go out with him. I mean, I know friendships are important, but I'm looking for Mr. Right, and right now that has to take precedence.

Sometimes things happen that are just weird. Tonight was just the night for it. First of all my brother Paul set me up again. I just realized that phrase means more than one thing.

Well, he set up a date for me to go out with Curt, who picked me up in a clown car. Well, technically, it's a smart car, but as we stuffed ourselves into it after he came to the door, it reminded me of the tiny kind where a bunch of clowns come rolling out at the circus. We rode in said clown car (they ride about like they look by the way in case any of you are thinking of buying one) to a couple of places. First we went to a recycling center and turned in some aluminum cans. I waited in the car, but I was still embarrassed for him. I mean it's pathetic enough that he has to do that to get enough money for a date, but you'd think he'd plan better and do it ahead of time. Then we went to the grocery store, where he turned in coins. Finally we went to Pasta Palace. I felt like I should dig around in my purse and pull out all of my spare change to contribute or maybe take him out since he's so down on his luck.

I like Pasta Palace. I probably wouldn't pick it for a date, but why not? Nobody's trying to impress anyone here. So as we sat there eating unlimited bread sticks and marinara sauce while we were waiting for our spaghetti, I asked Curt what he does.

"What do I do?" he asked, signaling for more free bread sticks.

"For a living," I said. Isn't that obvious? What else could I mean, do in your spare time? I already know what he does. He hunts for aluminum cans.

"I have a scrap metal collection business," he said.

Yep, just like I said, collects cans. "Aluminum?" I asked.

"All scrap metal," he said, "not just aluminum."

Well, more power to him. Too bad we didn't take my car; I have an empty pop can or two in there that I would have contributed. I didn't tell him, but I just throw away my empties. I may feel kind of guilty about that from now on.

Okay, so we came out of Pasta Palace, and drove the toy car to get dessert. Curt must like his desserts, because he had several coupons to choose from. He selected one for ice cream: buy one get one free sundaes. Well it's rare that I turn down a dessert, but I was full of bread sticks. I didn't want to be a party pooper, though, so we started toward Franky's Dessert Emporium. Ice cream shouldn't take up much room, right?

Ice cream may not be that filling, but a sundae is a whole other thing. I felt I deserved some mint chip anyway to make up for the scoops I lost on the cave man date. And it hit the spot with two scoops of mint chip with chocolate syrup, whipped cream, and a cherry on top.

Curt can spot the cans. He spied two in the grass when we came out with our sundaes, and it was dark by then. He nabbed them, putting the cans in a box in his trunk. It was a little embarrassing because there were other people eating outside at little tables with giant red umbrellas.

All the while I felt like everyone was watching us and talking about how Curt picked up the garbage. I tried to tell myself that he was actually helping Franky's employees with keeping up the lot, but I still felt

179

like people were probably feeling sorry for the girl who couldn't do better than a garbage picker.

So the date ended by ten. (Curt is an early bird.) I told him I had a nice time, and I did, and his job (or lack thereof) aside, he was another nice guy, but not anybody I can't live without.

I've lost count of how many times I said or thought that, and I'll admit it is beginning to seem like this experiment is a failure. Originally, I didn't set a number on how many dates I'd be willing to go on, and I haven't been keeping track, anyway. I thought my family, friends, and coworkers would have run out of options by now, honestly. I never thought I'd have gone on this many dates. And I've got another one tomorrow. I'm going to the county fair.

Good night, maybe I'll see you at the fair (although you won't know it's me). I'll be the one with the deep-fried Twinkie.

Chapter Nineteen

A lot of you commented that I shouldn't be so concerned with appearances (and you're right). Not only was Curt cleaning up the parking lot, but he was helping the environment, too. Those cans would have ended up in the landfill if not for Curt. Well, before I tell you about my county fair date that my brother Joshua arranged for me, let me tell you how wrong a girl can be.

I was talking to Paul about Curt, kind of in a "Thanks for setting me up with the dumpster diver guy" kidding sort of way. Um, he's a millionaire. Yeah, he's one of those closet millionaires who live like everyday people (or worse). He owns that recycling center where we dropped off the cans. So I totally blew it financially. I'm okay with that, though. I'm not looking for a millionaire, just a regular guy. Someone like that actually can be the opposite of what a girl wants. Who wants a husband who makes his kids hunt through the couch cushions for their weekly allowance?

But kidding aside, that borders on obsessive behavior. Then you get into all kinds of personality disorders like hoarding and stalking. There was a case in the news last month about some guy out west who was stalking a girl and practically killed her before he was through with her. No, I just want a regular, nice guy I'm attracted to. Is that so much to ask?

Well, it might be, because while we're speaking of obsessive compulsive behavior, let me tell you about Hunter, who took me to the county fair.

I know you're thinking "cheap date." Have you been to the fair? There is an admission fee, which to me is a rip-off. That's like paying to get into Wal-Mart. Once you get inside the gate, the only free thing is the country western singer that I would have readily skipped, but who Hunter wanted to see for some reason. They all sound alike to me. (Please don't write me about how you love country music. I don't hate it; I just don't love it. We can all agree to disagree on that one.)

You have to pay once you get in for everything from the fried Twinkie to the spin you around until you are sick tilt-a-whirl ride and everything in between. And other than fattening food and sickening rides, what is there to do? See the animals. Well, I'm sure that's fun if you have kids with you, but do I care which goat or heifer gets first place? They all look alike to a city girl.

And how do they pick the hottest day of the year for the fair? Do they consult the Farmer's Almanac in advance? It was exceptionally hot this year, and no girl looks good with sweat trickling down her face. I wanted to go into the air-conditioned exhibition hall since we were just biding our time until the country-western singer that Hunter liked was on stage.

I was biding my time. Hunter had other plans.

Hunter is a reasonably good-looking man. His brown hair is a little longer than I normally like on a guy. If it's longer than mine, we have a problem. His just kept getting in his eyes, which would have driven me crazy, personally. But I think Hunter might have already been partially there.

We stopped at a booth where you shoot fake ducks or something to win a prize (hence the tongue in cheek name: Hunter). At the beginning I wasn't paying attention to what he was doing because there was a lovely smell wafting from the kettle corn booth next door that was particularly distracting. By the end I was trying to distance myself from the whole thing.

So Hunter's first mistake was getting in a long line of people to do his duck shooting game. That is annoying. I avoid lines whenever possible. I pointed out to him that the line at the kettle corn booth was exceptionally short. He wasn't interested. Well, I was, and since I had a little mad money in my purse, I got in the short line and bought my own kettle corn. And yes, I ate the whole bag. "What happens at the fair, stays at the fair," including all pounds gained from salty/sweet snacks. That's my motto.

You have to hand it to a guy with this much focus. Hunter stuck it out to the front of the line, where I rejoined him to watch. Ping, ping and the game was over. You lost your money and got a consolation prize. What fun. Let's head to the exhibition hall.

But no. He had to play again. He had his eye on the prize, which was a large half squashed stuffed dog that looked like the man running the booth had been using it as a seat cushion. Hunter did better the second time, almost winning said dog. Okay, let's move along to the air conditioning now.

But no. Hunter had to play again. In matter of fact, he had to play until he won. I'd hate to go to Vegas with the guy, because he just couldn't stop. He tried changing guns. He tried another angle. He did everything short of putting his longish dark brown hair in an updo to get it out of his eyes. The man emptied his wallet; then he accused the guy who was running the booth of cheating. Seems the sights on the guns were bent or twisted; maybe it was the gun barrel. I know now it was the user who was twisted. There was quite a ruckus. The police were not called, but he almost got his behind tossed out of the fair because he would not get out of line and let some other sucker give away his money for a cheap piece of

you massacre your county fair prize and spread it all over the girl's lawn.

But no.

* * *

Many of you seemed to feel you'd had the same kind of experience, since you've been teepeed. I don't know if you can rightly compare picking fluff out of grass with pulling toilet paper off tree limbs. I've never been teepeed. I wasn't going for first prize in this anyway, okay? Then several of you got carried away. You people need to stop posting your stories of worst pranks ever played on you. You're giving people ideas. I can't keep this up, deleting your posts. I'm a working girl, you know.

I was in the middle of describing my stalker. So nothing else happened for a couple of days. I thought I was free of Hunter. Then I got the card.

No return address, but I opened it without a second thought. Inside was one of those thinking of you cards with puppies (carrying through the fair prize dog theme, I guess), only a big red line was drawn through it at an angle like it was a do not enter street sign, and inside was a nice little typed note accusing me of everything under the sun with numerous men. I swear I didn't tell him about my blind date experiment! Maybe he got wind of my blog somehow. He hasn't commented on here, though.

Anyway, the card and note were just threatening enough that I was starting to get a little scared. I took them to the police station. The officers asked if he'd ever hurt me, and I told them about how he grabbed me at the fair and showed them the bruise. They took a picture; it's starting to fade. They said I should have snapped a shot of it when it first appeared. Well, sure, that's one for the scrapbook; what was I thinking to skip that great photo op?

Anyway, long story short, I had to take off work and go to court to get a restraining order against him. He, of course, is protesting his innocence. Yes we know, Hunter, and prisons are full of innocent men packed in like sardines.

So there you have it. I don't think Hunter is dangerous. He's just a nuisance. The restraining order should put the fear of God into him, or at least the fear of the law.

Prayers are appreciated.

Chapter Twenty

Trent needed a ride to pick his car up from the dealer today. I forgot what was wrong with it. Usually dealers are just a ripoff, but there's a Honda dealer in our town that isn't too bad.

I arrived early at the school, so I walked over to the playground to watch the kids. They've got cool gym equipment now. It looks like they're training kids to go on American Ninja Warrior. These kids are pretty impressive, swinging from wheel to wheel ten feet off the ground. And if they don't stick the landing, they roll like Olympic gymnasts. I think they're made of rubber.

Trent teaches second grade. He had his group of kids out there. He's great with them. Schools could use more like him.

The only male teacher I had in elementary school was sixth grade - Mr. Jones. He was grim. Really grim. The man should not have been a teacher. I think I heard he left the profession the year after I was in his class. He was always sending notes home to my parents. "Annika talks too much in class," was one I got almost every week. Another frequent one was "Annika has trouble accepting criticism." I think what he actually wanted to say was "Annika is mouthy, and I'm ready to join the Peace

Corp to escape her." I swear I was kidding most of the time! My parents did what they could, but you know every kid has his or her bent, and my sense of humor was already twisted by then.

Back to Trent, so he's out there playing with the kids. He was calling them his little monsters and they were growling and jumping on his back. It took several of them to bring him down, but they did it. Then, growling, he threw them off, and they all chased him around the schoolyard.

It's too bad that the romance just isn't there with Trent. He's going to make someone, probably Brooke, a wonderful husband and a great dad to her son.

I walked back to my car and pulled up in front of the school to wait for him. I heard a bell ring, and the kids shot out like whipped cream dispensed from a can. You've got to agree that whipped cream in a can is one of the greatest inventions of all time. Can you imagine having to whip it up every time you had pie or wanted to make a sundae? It's good straight from the can, too.

Brooke was waiting for her son, also. I can never remember his name. She looked perfect, of course. Maybe it's a requirement when you work in cosmetics to always look gorgeous. I wondered why she wasn't giving Trent a ride. Maybe she had to get to work. Her son came out, climbed in her car, and she left. When all the kids were gone, Trent came out.

"You look nice," I said. He had on a button-down shirt and tie. "The other teachers aren't that dressed up." I'd seen several on the playground. I don't blame them. They work with sticky kids all day.

"I think it's important to give children something bigger to shoot for. They have enough people in their lives in jeans and t-shirts."

"Yeah," I said; then I was silent, considering. Brooke must be on her way to work, and why she looked perfect and couldn't give her near-fiancé Trent a ride. I wondered if they'd be tying the knot soon. Trent of course noticed my uncharacteristic quietness.

"What's wrong?" he asked.

"Nothing," I lied. What was I supposed to say? I was watching you with those kids and wishing there was something between us just because I want a husband and children? Um, that's slightly insulting. I mean, not the part about him making a good dad, but I wouldn't want a man to pick me just because he thought I'd be a good mom to his children.

It was a quiet trip. When I dropped him off, he leaned in the car and said, "We should go out sometime."

For a moment I thought he meant for something other than Chinese, but then he said, "I haven't had my regular dose of MSG in a while." I laughed, but it still seemed strange to agree. I used to have a boyfriend who would say "we ought to go out," then never carry through. Of course, that guy meant on a real date.

Trent continued, "I can't this week, though. I promised Brooke I'd go on a picnic with her and Joel."

Joel! That's his name! I don't know why it's so hard to remember. We agreed to go next Wednesday, and I drove away.

A picnic is so romantic. It might not be with a child along, but it still sounded fun. I could picture it with a checkered tablecloth on the ground, and Trent and Joel playing ball off to the side while Brooke set out the food. They'd probably have cold fried chicken or maybe just some sandwiches. I don't know if she is much of a cook...

Someone honked at me. I'd sat through the green arrow and completely missed it. How embarrassing! There were a whole line of people behind me honking. Well, there was nothing I could do about it now. I rolled my window down and waved an apology. Then I made sure my windows were up and my doors locked in case someone back there wanted to come have a little talk with me.

So now KFC sounded good to me. Go figure. I hit the drive-thru and ordered a two-piece meal. Have you noticed that the pieces have shrunk? The thought occurred to me that poultry farmers must be slaughtering them younger. So I'm eating baby chickens? Ugh! I threw the rest away and just finished the biscuit, mashed potatoes, and coleslaw.

I started to head toward home, but why? Grace was never there anymore. I was close to the mall, so I pulled into the Macy's lot. I always park there. If you pick a new spot each time, it's hard to find your car. Also, it's usually vacant, and they have a handy restroom.

Anyway, as I passed by the cosmetics counter, there was Brooke. So I was right. She was on her way to work. She saw me and waved me over. I couldn't pretend I didn't notice, so I dragged myself over.

Would you be able to keep from comparing yourself to her? I couldn't help it. Me with my supersonic shoulder-length hair, her with her long, flowing, perfectly straight coif. She is elegant. I am not. We chatted for a couple of minutes about makeup. She had some pointers. I didn't want to have her fuss with my face; for all I knew I still had some chicken grease on it. I wiped my mouth with my hand. I didn't see any, but you never know. I couldn't think of a reason to decline, though.

I have to admit; when she was done, I looked more sophisticated and I don't know... brighter? Maybe I overdo the muted tones, if that makes sense.

I surveyed myself in the mirror. She asked me if I'd ever considered straightening my hair. I wasn't insulted. A lot of people suggest this. I've done it a couple of times in the past, though, and I looked like a penguin. With this makeup job and straight hair, I'd look like a sophisticated penguin... still not what I'm going for.

I said this. She smiled. She studied me.

"You know what would look great on your lips? Perfect Peach." She pulled out a cardboard strip with a sparkly peach color and held it up to my face. It looked like it would be a pretty shade on me.

Great, a cheap way to update my look. I started to get out my credit card.

She looked around in a drawer on her side of the counter. "I don't have any in stock."

I was disappointed. I was looking forward to a new lip color.

She jabbed her finger in the air. "I have one in my car that I was going to give to my friend for her birthday in a couple of days, but I could give her another color. It'd look better on you. We could run out there now. I'm due for a break."

I agreed; she had another saleswoman cover her counter and we left.

She's hard to keep up with. She's several inches taller than I am, so she makes better time, glides really, but still looks elegant. I had to take almost two steps to each one of hers. I looked like a toddler trying to keep up with mommy. I didn't want to complain, though, because it was nice of her to take her break to do that for me.

She unlocked her trunk, and while she rooted around for my purchase, I stared at the painting that was taking up most of the space. You couldn't ignore it. I had to pull the portrait out.

"May I?" I asked.

"What? Oh, sure."

It was of Trent. He was staring at me with that silly grin he wears when he's teasing. She'd captured it perfectly.

"It's for his mom. It's her birthday tomorrow."

I nodded. His mom probably loved Brooke. She'd never cared much for me. There was always a puzzled look on her face when I talked, like she was wondering why I bothered. She usually ended up nodding politely like she hadn't heard a thing I'd said, which was probably true.

"How much do I owe you?" I asked still staring at the painting.

"It'll be $19.98 with tax," she said.

I put Trent back in the trunk. She closed it. I fumbled around in my purse for my wallet, pulled out a twenty, and handed it to her.

"Thanks, I've got to get going," I said.

"No problem," she said and glided back to the store.

Well, Trent was right. Brooke was very talented. I could probably wipe up the floor with Brooke when it came to spreadsheets and reports. Of course no one except your boss cares about something like that, and even then only if you mess up or are late with one or the other. I'd always wanted to be artistic. I guess Brooke was pretty much perfect.

I went home, dropped the makeup in my bag, and got out a pint of chocolate-covered almonds in coffee ice cream that I'd bought the day before. I hope Grace didn't want any of that, because it magically disappeared. That's a single-serving container, right?

Chapter Twenty-one

I haven't been on here for several days, sorry. You know how busy a working girl can get.

It sounds like we all love fried chicken. It's one of the few leftovers you can eat cold, that's better than when it was hot. I might not be able to stomach it for a while, now, after my last meal of midget chickens.

Several of you said I shouldn't compare myself with others. No one is perfect, even Brooke. I guess all she needs is to be perfect for Trent, anyway, and it's obvious she is.

And thank you for the outpouring of concern, but these tricks are nothing but venting from Hunter. Annikawhatareyouthinking has posted several times about his or her worry. Trust me, I can handle this. Maybe you should take a breather from this blog if it is making you that uneasy, dear, because the game continues.

I had to read the fine print to see how restraining my order was, but it covers just about everything... even baked goods in this case. I have to hand it to Hunter, he's a little more sophisticated than I gave him credit for and more mean-spirited. He sent me a dessert at work... a tart.

Lemon tart to be specific. So, what is he trying to say here? I'm a tart tart? It came with an unsigned card that had "missing you" scratched out and "I never miss" written inside.

Threatening card notwithstanding, it's too bad I'm afraid of being poisoned. I wouldn't have minded a little lemon tart. We gave it to the police to have it analyzed. I found out later I could have eaten it. Don't you hate it when your stalker sends you a perfectly good dessert, and you waste it? Now that he's planted the suggestion, I really want lemon tart.

The police tracked it to a little Danish bakery. I'm surprised there are bakeries that deliver something so small. It was paid for over the phone with a prepaid Visa card, untraceable. The police couldn't prove Hunter was the one who sent it, so they said there wasn't anything they could do about it other than pull him in for questioning. He denied it, of course.

It is disturbing that he is continuing this weirdness, and disappointing. After getting the restraining order on him, I felt like I could relax until this happened.

So I still need to be on my guard, but I'm not going to sit around locked up in my house afraid to answer the door because some guy likes to play tricks. John set up a blind date for me with a new friend of his for tonight,   and I went.

We had a great time at a little Italian place downtown. Now I was told to wear something comfortable for the thing we were going to do afterward, so I wore jeans. That's just about as comfortable as you can get without wearing sweats. Turned out I should have worn sweats. After stuffing myself with pasta, Tony drove to a place that wasn't far: A Little Piece of Heaven. Well, you can imagine what was going through my head with a name like that. My first thought, of course, was dessert and that I wish I'd worn the sweats because I was so stuffed I'd have a hard time eating anything else. I didn't want any buttons popping or zippers giving way. I wish I could tell you that I didn't say this aloud, but I did. Tony has a good sense of humor. So, we laughed together when he said it was a rock climbing place.

Then I realized he'd just said the words "rock climbing." I was ready to do some climbing... right back into the car. No way was I going to hang by a hook and ropes while I scrambled up a fake rock wall. I didn't want to ruin his evening, though, so I didn't say anything. I followed along.

When you get inside it's all primary colors; it reminded me of a preschool. Maybe that is to make it seem less threatening, more fun. As soon as I walked in and saw kids climbing with no trouble, I thought, "How hard can this be?"

So sure, I wasn't dressed right, and I'm a little plump and don't have much muscle, but if some little kids can do it, so can I, right?

Only one problem with that thinking: children are limber little monkeys; I am not. I wish I'd remembered that fact before I climbed the wall.

So there is a belayer there who Tony knows. They're good friends. A belayer is someone who makes sure you don't fall. So, while Tony was on the ground directing me where to put my feet and hands, the belayer was controlling the rope that is attached to me. When I got to the top, it was exhilarating. To be honest, I didn't think I could climb all the way up.

I was all set to go down when I realized they moved the floor. In fact, they moved it several scary feet down. I wouldn't say I was paralyzed with fear, but I couldn't move. Between Tony and his friend talking to me and lowering me down slowly, I landed safely. I'd say I kissed the floor, but again, that's disgusting, but I wanted to.

Tony was good about the whole thing, but there's a whole world of difference between being a good sport, and meshing. We didn't mesh. So I bid Tony an early good night and ended up in my pjs in front of the TV with a dish of moose tracks again. I'm sure I burned up at least that many calories sweating through the terror alone!

* * *

A few of you mentioned that I should take my weight a little more seriously. I'm only a little out of shape and a bit plump, people. I'm thirty. I'm not going to have a heart attack from climbing a rock wall! But I am not holding that against you, because you don't know me very well, and I use a little hyperbole now and then for emphasis.

On the way to work today, I stopped and bought a lemon tart. I got a mini one, just to satisfy my craving. It was good. I highly recommend them.

I'm busy at work now since it's audit time, but I'm going to dash this off just to keep you up to date (no pun intended). I'll tell you about the stalker first; then my most recent date.

First my brother Joshua stopped by the office to apologize about Hunter. He feels bad. I guess he didn't know him very well; certainly not well enough to fix him up with his sister. From now on, I'm making sure my siblings and friends know these guys well, or it's auf wiedersehen, buddy.

Right after Josh left, I had to run home to get some paperwork I'd been working on the night before that I'd forgotten. There was a box on my front porch with a card on top. The card had little bunnies hopping all over the front and inside was the message, "You're no bunny 'til some bunny loves you!" It was not signed.

I did not open the box. I called the police. I was afraid to move it. Anything could have been in there. The police told me not to open it, anyway, when I called them. Well, I hate to tell you, but a bomb squad arrived!

It was surreal. I stood outside the police tape perimeter while a team of experts handled it. Everything seemed to move in slow motion; it took so long before we found out the contents of the box. Inside was something awful though not dangerous: a stuffed bunny with fake blood on it and a knife through its heart! I felt a little silly that the bomb squad was called in, but the police had no other choice. They checked it for fingerprints, but there weren't any. They couldn't prove it came from Hunter.

And now I am actually afraid. Before I just thought it was a nuisance more than anything. All along a lot of you have left comments that I should be taking this more seriously and shouldn't joke about it, and you're right. It's no laughing matter. Grace and I moved back in with our parents, but I'm still uneasy.

I'll tell you, I've never prayed so hard in my life as I have since Hunter started hounding me. But I know I have to put my life in the hands of my Father and live it while being aware of the possibility of danger at any time. Other than the bruise on my arm, he hasn't hurt me physically. I thought at the time he didn't mean to do it. Shows how wrong a girl can be.

In the day we live in, danger is always a real possibility for everyone. But does that mean we have to close ourselves off from the rest of the world? If we do, then evil wins. Live I must, so... on to the next date.

Adam picked me up from my parents' house at 6:00. We didn't say anything newsworthy in the car, just the usual trading of occupation info and things like that. I noticed right away that the man checks his phone at every stoplight. We reached Kai Tiki and got a booth near the front window, which helps a lot since the place could use quite a few more tiki torches. Maybe Kai Tiki means "no tiki." If we hadn't been sitting near a window, I wouldn't have been able to read my menu.

Some people might consider that a very romantic atmosphere with the mood lighting and all. It's not needed on a first date, though. In fact, wouldn't it be nice to see who you're talking to, see what you're getting into? We didn't need any extra light, after ordering though, because Adam was getting all he needed from his phone. He was deeply into a baseball game. Really? Come on... those players must have been a quarter of an inch high. He kept checking stats and watching highlights.

I've seen people who go out to eat and sit there not talking, looking at their phones, but not at each other. I never thought it would happen to me. I refused to pull out my phone. I tried to engage Adam in conversation, but the inane baseball game was just so exciting that he had to keep returning to it. When the food came, I ate quickly while he took bites in between highlights.

As soon as I was finished eating, I suggested we leave. Adam wasn't anywhere near done, so he looked a bit surprised. I don't think it even occurred to him that he was being rude by ignoring me so much with his stupid device. I think that's his life... constant distraction. He needs to figure this out on his own. I didn't even try to make an excuse why I wanted to go.

At the end of the evening, I considered giving Martin's information to Adam since they're both sports buffs; they could have gone to a game together. I might have found him his new best friend!

Chapter Twenty-two

A lot of you agreed with me about the cell phone problem, but others insist this is the age we live in. I know it is. That's my point. "Wherever you are, be all there," as Jim Elliot said. Think about it, people.

I always mean to keep these blog posts short, but I usually have so much to tell you. Today is no different, so bear with me. It may take a few days of posts for me to share what's been happening at work and all.

I don't know how many dates Nadine had with our boss, Jack, because I never brought it up with her. Some things are just better left unsaid. Especially since we have to work together. I thought she looked guilty though, and she didn't come into my office unless she had to for at least a week. Maybe I'm wrong. Maybe I should have said something. Jack is so not worth ruining a good working relationship and friendship.

Anyway, so there we all were, working awkwardly together,. Nadine and Jack hiding their relationship from me, and I was hiding the fact that I knew they were hiding their relationship from me, and work was going on like usual... I guess.

Then it came time for the yearly audit.

Normally these are just a formality. We always balance. We're a non-profit, so we want to always be above reproach in money matters. We also try to keep administration costs down, using donations wisely, and we're very transparent about finances so we normally welcome the outside audit. This year the figures didn't add up.

As the accountant, I am, of course, responsible for the count, so when it didn't come out right, I was checking and rechecking figures. You cannot imagine unless you work with numbers how obsessed I am with this. I can't figure it out! I knew it had to just be a clerical error. I'm still wracking my brain for how this could have happened, and I need to find the answer before the auditors return to reexamine the books. I'll keep you updated.

I skipped a date in there somewhere. We went to dinner and a movie. I forgot which one and who I was with, but I saw Trent there with Brooke. I didn't get a chance to say "hi." We haven't seen each other lately. I guess he's busy with Brooke. They've been dating for a while. They'll probably be getting engaged soon. Not sure how I feel about that, or how Brooke would feel about her fiancé or husband going out weekly with another woman.

Maybe that's not a good term to use: another woman.

Anyway on to my next date. Lydia arranged this one. How many of you like to go swimming? Or perhaps you don't especially care for it? I fall into this category. I don't hate the water. I don't love it, but when I was given the opportunity to go to the Swim Club, I jumped at the chance.

It was located across from the high school I attended way back when, and it was just beautiful. I know... Swim Club is such an understated name. It cost so much that my parents never even considered joining. It fell into the category of one of those kind of things where you looked through the fence (literally) with adolescent eyes wondering what it would be like to sip smoothies by the pool on a hot July day looking like a swimsuit model. Maybe I even thought at the time that joining would make my slightly plump self more athletic with all of that swimming, although as far as I could see there was more lounging going on than anything.

The day dawned with a high expected in the 90s. That's pretty hot for our part of the country. Perfect, I thought. The cool water will feel good. The ice-cold delicious smoothie will be just what I need on such a hot day. My date, Kyle, told Lydia he'd meet me there. The rendezvous spot was the diving board at 3:00. Kyle had put my name in at the front desk, and I had no problem getting in when I arrived. I changed into my suit and headed for the water.

The pool area was all that I imagined it to be. The chaise lounges beckoned more than the water, and I was tempted to stretch out luxuriously in the sun since I was a few minutes early. Besides, there was a deeply tanned guy hanging around the diving board in a suit that was so skimpy that I felt embarrassed for him. Most of the men there were wearing the longer suits. I decided to wait until he moved on to take my place at the appointed spot.

I shook out my towel and lay down on the lounge chair. It was as comfortable as I imagined it would be. Everything would have been perfect, like I'd always known it would be back when I was fourteen, if only I had a smoothie. After a few minutes, I was starting to get really warm. I hadn't brought any money with me, no pockets in the suit and all. But I went over and looked at the smoothie menu anyway. The luscious looking Extreme Meme Berry had three kinds of berries in it. I wondered if they would put banana in that if I asked.

It was a few minutes after 3, but that guy with the skimpy suit was still hanging around the board. I looked around to see if there were any unattached guys who could be Kyle when the realization hit me. Skimpy Suit *was* Kyle! I looked back at him. He was talking to several young things in equally skimpy suits. That couldn't be him... could it?

It could. I went over to him and introduced myself. Now you might as well know that I was wearing what I thought was a cute one-piece, a brilliant blue with polka dots and with... okay with a skirt, but it was short!

I gathered from the way his smile froze on his face that I was not what he expected. Well, that made two of us. I've never hung out with a guy wearing a bikini.

He was polite, though. We settled down on a couple of chairs and started to talk. Yeah, we talked, but I couldn't tell you what color his eyes were with his face averted looking at every girl who passed by wearing a suit that, as my mother would say, left nothing to the imagination.

Which was every woman in the place, except me. They were tanned, too, with a tan that must have penetrated every layer down to the bone. Some day they're going to regret that, but right now, their deep, wrinkle-inducing copper looked much better my lily white skin.

I'll admit all of this in my blog, but let me tell you that while I was sitting there on that chaise lounge with a guy who was looking everywhere but at me, I felt very conspicuous because I didn't lack clothing. Yes! I stuck out because I wasn't bare enough! What a world.

So pretty soon, Kyle suggested he'd love to teach me to dive. I already know how to dive, but there wasn't anything else going on. No smoothies were being offered, so I agreed.

At first, Kyle was giving me pointers, correcting my stance, showing off his diving abilities from the high dive, and I was fine with all of that. He's actually quite artistic. But then he started drawing a crowd.

Did I forget to say that Kyle is muscular? He's quite impressive with his fancy dives, too, so I can understand the crowd of onlookers, even people wanting pointers on how to dive like Kyle. But did they all have to be women?

And Kyle was so obliging. He was happy to teach each and every female there the finer points of diving. I'll tell you what; those rich, bikini-clad women can be pushy. Pretty soon, I was just a polka-dotted outsider on the outskirts of the diving lesson circle.

It didn't take very long for me to have enough of that. I tried get close enough to Kyle to say good bye, but I couldn't get through without pushing several women out of the way. That's not how I roll, so I rolled on out of there.

I called Lydia on the way home to find out why a guy like that would want to go on a blind date. I'm sure he could get all the dates he wanted just by showing off at pools. Lydia said he was new in town. Okay, whatever.

Some of you will want to comment on this post, saying if I just lost weight, I could fit my slightly plump self into a skimpy suit and fit in with all of the other barely-there swimwear. Let me set the record straight. I actually like this suit. I would still wear it even if I lost 20 pounds (well, wear one a size or two smaller), because it is pretty modest (for a swimsuit) yet still cute.

You're right about losing weight, though. I need to stop complaining about being a few pounds over and do something about it. Right after I order myself a smoothie.

* * *

Let me set everyone straight. I am not obsessed with smoothies as some of you seem to believe. I'm obsessed with sugar. But since I refused to be controlled by an addiction once I've faced the fact that I have one, let the record show that on this day, I have cut out sugar until I lose some weight.

So, to substitute, every time I want a delectable sweet, I'm drinking something instead. Now, I know that theoretically it should be water, because everything else has calories (Do not say the words diet soda to me or I'll have to delete your comment. That stuff is evil.), but what kind of substitute is water for say, a triple berry smoothie? No, I'm having coffee. Now, don't write to me and tell me that coffee is addicting too. I already drink coffee, and I'm not addicted to it.

Okay, back to the work situation. I told you in my last post that the numbers were not adding up. First perhaps, I should tell you the problem was a lack of money in our account. I balanced just last month, so I went over and over the figures for this month. I have a meeting later this week with the bank's customer service department to go over all of the deposits that have gone through our account. I'm hoping it's a clerical error on their part. It's almost never a banking error, though, so I'd rather find it myself than have one of their employees point out where I've made a mistake.

Until then I'll tell you about the last date I had; my brother, Paul, set up this one. Since you might not have caught on yet, my work ethic is strong. If I am not truly sick with a fever, vomiting, or something debilitating, I am at work. I rarely take my vacation days. I'd be embarrassed to tell you how many days I have banked, because I know downtime is important, but suffice to say that when a date required taking a day off like this next one did, especially with the books not balancing, I was tempted to suggest another time, perhaps another year, but I already have the appointment scheduled to go over our accounts with the bank. I've been concentrating so hard on solving this problem, so I decided a little r and r was just the thing to take my mind off of my work dilemma.

I don't know what I expected we would do, but honestly fishing never occurred to me.

Chapter Twenty-three

A lot of you said I was probably overreacting to the swimsuit thing. One of you even said you like me the way I am. That's sweet, except you have no idea what I look like.

No, I'm still cutting out sugar. It's best to go cold turkey with sneaky, addictive substances like that, so no more smoothies, moose tracks, candy, kettle corn, cake or pies. Nope, no tarts either.

This was my first date ever to end at Urgent Care. Before I go any further, I would like to throw this out there: I never claimed to be a fishing expert. If you set up a date with a woman who lacks fishing know-how, be ready for, well, anything.

My lack of knowledge also included not knowing what to wear. I would recommend if any of you are considering going fly-fishing, don't wear jeans and tennis shoes. Actually I'd advise against going at all, but that could just be my bias talking.

So I showed up at six a.m. at Sugar Creek (just what I needed - a reminder that I'm off sugar) as instructed by Colin's voice mail. I'd tried to call him back to get more information when I heard the message he'd left, but he didn't answer the phone, maybe because it was after nine when

I called. I guess the guy was trying to get in his beauty rest before he got up at the crack of dawn. And why get up so early? To surprise the fish? I decided that maybe in the vein of "the early bird gets the worm" he wanted to get to the tackle shop before all of the good worms were gone.

Yeah, so I'm stumbling around, yawning all over myself on the banks of Sugar Creek promptly at six, but he's not there. He'd left pretty easy instructions on where to meet, so I was sure I wasn't at the wrong place. I didn't even bring coffee figuring that would necessitate visiting a restroom, and who knew if there would even be one! Let me tell you, fishing is more complicated than it sounds.

He finally arrived around 6:20 mumbling something about insomnia. I can identify with having trouble sleeping, so that part was easy to forgive. What wasn't so easy was how seriously the man took fishing. He gave a brief demonstration of fly-fishing; then I was expected to stop making any noise. As in no talking. Seriously, the man expected complete and total silence... from me.

Also, right off the bat I was wrong about the worms showing up for our little excursion, which relieved me to no end. I'll pick up a dirty, slimy worm if needed, but I'd rather not have to. And impale it on a hook and then drown it? Not interested.

We were fly-fishing. I know that sounds even worse, but don't

216

worry, they don't use real flies. They're lures and Colin was wearing them on his hat like they were decorations. Colin produced a fly for each of us guaranteed to catch the eye of the most timid trout. He "tied" them himself and seemed quite proud of them. That's probably the mark of a true angler, if he's willing to not only use the ugly as sin fly he made and but also hand one over to a woman like it's a present. It was a true mess with tons of knotted thread. They name these flies sometimes. Mine I have christened the Bug-eyed Mangler. I thought it was clever. I even included the word angler in there, kind of. I didn't think Colin would appreciate my humor, so I kept that to myself. Also, by that time we'd reached the silent part of the fishing trip, so sharing wasn't allowed.

There's another interesting term: trip. I took it a little too literally. We weren't there very long before the combination of incorrect shoes, bottom muck, and algae-covered rocks had me sitting on the floor of Sugar Creek.

Funny thing about that name Sugar. It sure didn't live up to its name. It evokes sweetness, happiness, perhaps even cookies home made by your mother. Oh, but Sugar was a fast creek, brassy and loud; someone who wouldn't care if you fell on your tush. She'd laugh uproariously without giving you a hand up.

I certainly didn't blame the creek for laughing, I'm sure I looked humorous, but Colin didn't even smile. The whole thing was awkward, like he somehow blamed me for lacking the grace to fall without splashing and scaring away the fish. So, no sense of humor... I've found that having one helps when life inevitably trips you and lands you on your tuchis. Laugh with each other; laugh at yourselves. I did. He should have too, at least a little.

When I was done with my solo, he made us move upstream since all of the splashing had ruined the fishing there.

The next spot was just as slippery, but I managed to keep my feet under me this time. Is there anything worse to wear than wet jeans? They were already wet to the knees because one has to wade into the water to fly fish. Did I forget to mention that? Sorry, I forgot that not everyone has seen "A River Runs Through It." That would have a good name for this blog entry.

Well, you know me; Annika always tries to be a good sport on these dates, so I already wasn't complaining about the wet jeans and walking around in my tennies going squish squish with every step. Technically what came next was my fault: I hooked Colin, and no I don't mean he was interested in me.

Unfortunately, an actual hook was embedded. You're probably hoping as I did that it was in that gosh-awful hat, but no, it had to be his ear. And if it had been an inch lower, he could've had a good start on some ear piercing, if he was into that sort of thing. And no, he wasn't.

I blame that whole ten-two thing that you're supposed to do while you're casting. You're just asking to get a barbed hook embedded in your ear swinging a pole around like that over and over. Also, when Colin explained his theories on fly fishing, something like hopper, copper, dropper, whopper, I floated away on a bobber of Dr. Seuss's Fox in Sox, sir (silently, of course). So, none of it actually reached my brain.

Fortunately, I caught on right away when he started screaming, that something was up, so I stopped with the pole swinging before he lost part of an ear. But there was blood. You may remember I am not good with any bodily fluids. Blood is the worst. I didn't faint, but maybe Colin would have preferred I did. I think he didn't want to be beholden to me. I'm the one who had to clip the line with my fingernail clippers (while trying not to look at the actual bloody hook, which is quite tricky) and get him to Urgent Care with a towel held against his head. I pulled the towel out of my trunk and didn't have time to remember if this was the same towel that Darrin drooled on. Let's just not go there.

The Urgent Care doc assured me they get this kind of thing happening all the time. Colin was not happy to be part of that demographic. He's none too chatty except when explaining the finer points of fly-fishing, so you can imagine how the three-hour wait went.

Me: So, what do you do for a living?

Colin: (Pretends he can't hear through the dirty towel on his head.)

Me: I'm an accountant.

Colin: (Pretends I don't exist.)

Me: I guess you must already know that.

Colin: (Pretends he's in his happy place, closes eyes, hums

tunelessly.)

And so we draw the curtain on another glamorous day in the life of

Annika Nordstrom.

* * *

The cold I caught from Sugar Creek went a long way toward

easing the guilt about the whole fishing incident. Summer colds are unfair.

At least with a winter one, staying home, bundled under the covers sipping

chicken noodle soup feels good. In the summer, it just makes you sweat.

Life goes on in the summer, and you can't stay home, no matter how much

your nose drips. For some reason everyone seems intent on convincing me

this is an allergy. I don't have allergies. Please don't leave comments

below on that. It's a cold.

One reader commented that by the end of these dates I won't set foot outside my house, because of all of the disasters. As I said in the beginning, I am a little uptight, but I've never been so much so that I'd barricade myself in my house. I'm embracing the world more than ever. Especially since my stalker seems to have found a new interest in life. It's always a good day when the stalker moves on. Grace and I are back in our house.

We had to face our fears with the stalker. It made us more aware of our surroundings and the people around us. We've relied more on God, each other, and our family than we have for a long time.

I'll admit something else on here since it's anonymous. It's looking more likely that I'll be an old maid. Is that even a term people use anymore? I want to get married. I want to have children. I never saw myself being alone my whole life like Miss Martha.

To be truthful, since none of these dates have worked out, I'm starting to wonder if it's me. I'm afraid to count how many dates I've been on the last few months, and I'm just not connecting with these guys. Some of them it's obvious why... they're freaks! But a few of the others are nice, normal guys who just are not interested in me or vice versa. What am I doing wrong or not doing right? Why aren't I connecting with them? I think I'm pretty transparent, but maybe it's only on this blog and with friends and family that I share who I really am. Maybe I'm so worried about being polite and being a good sport that I've hidden... me. Maybe it's just the cold talking. I feel lousy.

Regarding the audit. I've moved up my meeting with the bank because I found out the auditors have scheduled a review for the first part of next week. I'm giving myself just a couple of more days. Still hoping it's a clerical error on the part of the bank. I went over the accounts again line by line. I've even examined other months, too, although I don't see how it could have happened then. I've always balanced every month. I'm in a real quandary. I need to figure out what happened, and I have to do it fast before the auditors return. I also need to talk to Jack about how the books haven't balanced. I've been putting it off, hoping I could find the error, but I'm going to have to talk to him about it today.

When I came into work yesterday morning, there was a box of chocolates on my desk. I didn't bother asking Zoe where they came from. I'm sure they're from Jack, because they're the same kind as last time. Does the man think he can get back into my good graces with chocolate? I'm not eating them. I offered him a couple when he dropped off a report today. He didn't say anything about them, but I see them as a bribe. Sugar has no power over me! (I've been repeating that to myself all day.) I set the rest of them on the back of my credenza as a self-discipline and am ignoring them. I swear I could smell them all day yesterday and today, though.

I've learned something about coffee. The more you drink it, the more you want to, perhaps even have to, drink it. I'm not saying I'm addicted, but I've about doubled my coffee consumption since I gave up sweets. I've lost 3 pounds though, so I'm going to keep up what I'm doing.

* * *

Well, I met with Jack, and it did not go well. I probably should have straightened it out with the people at the bank first. It could still be an error on their part. Jack got on my case! He basically told me that I would have to replace the money if I can't find it, or criminal proceedings would be brought against me! Would they do that? I don't understand. I'm so careful. How could I be this inept? I didn't steal anything!

And boy, has Jack changed! No more touchy feely Smooth as Silk Guy. He's more like Sandpaper Man. He sure rubbed me the wrong way. It's kind of surprising. He's being quite unprofessional.

I was already having a bad day, so being talked to like that was the last thing I needed. I awakened from a nightmare and couldn't fall back asleep the night before. I blame it on the pizza and the classics.

I decided to finally read some of the classical literature that my family have been giving me every Christmas and birthday. I'd taken an American Literature class in college and spouted off how superior that writing was over today's stuff. We read short stories in the class. I could get through those with no trouble, but the novels were... well, long. I'm not that much of a reader anyway. I suppose I could have just told everyone I wasn't getting into them as much as I'd hoped, but I didn't.

So I determined to read them, picking one at random... The House of the Seven Gables. Wouldn't you know the first one I'd pick would have a pathetic old maid in it? I'm barely into it, but I've fixated on poor Hepizbah Pyncheon now. Not only is she practically alone in that big old scary house, but she sure didn't age well in Hawthorne's tale. After reading the description of her, I examined every line, real or imagined, in my face in a magnifying mirror and plastered my crow's feet with lotion before I went to bed.

I'd had pizza for supper, too. That always gives me nightmares. I dreamed I lived in the House of the Seven Gables, and I was Hepzibah, a crusty old woman with creaky limbs dressed in a ghostly white nightgown and nightcap. I was trying to escape the house, but I could barely get out of bed.

When I finally managed to drag myself out (in my dream), I wandered from room to spooky room, carrying a lone candle with a tiny flame that gave almost no light. I tugged fitfully on each door, the rusty hinges squeaking in protest. Each door just led to another room. I couldn't find the front door! Some voice in the background kept saying "Give her blood to drink! Give her blood to drink!"

I finally reached the front door, but before I could open it, a gust of wind blew my candle out, and I couldn't find the door handle. Suddenly a trapdoor opened up, and I felt myself falling. I hit bottom on a dirt floor in a dark dungeon. The only light came from a small table with a candelabra, which I picked up. I finally saw the door and took a few steps toward it, but it was blocked by a skeleton reaching toward me with a bony hand!

I screamed, and it must have woke me up. I was never so glad to escape a dream in my life. I'm going to rethink my pizza consumption since it seems to cause nightmares, and I'm giving that book away. The old maid part was bad enough, but drink blood? You know how I feel about bodily fluids. I had to take Tums and have two cups of cocoa, and even then I didn't get much sleep.

Chapter Twenty-four

I can't remember the last time Trent and I went out for Chinese. We went tonight, though, and it is Trent's and my last Chinese together. He broke the code. No, he didn't date my boss, if that's what you're thinking. It was a different code and worse. He saw something secret that I didn't want him to see.

I'm sure you can't imagine that I have any secrets left after all of the soul-baring I've done on here, but I do. Of course, this is all anonymous, so no one knows this is me.

I've kept a few items from my high school and college years put away in my bedroom. They're in something that I wouldn't call a "hope chest" so much as a "chest of remembrances," mementos of past relationships. This consists of a locked trunk at the foot of my bed. It's actually quite decorative. It's a studded wooden steamer trunk, and I drape a brightly colored velvet throw over one end.

It contains all of the things I wouldn't show anyone. No one looks inside, not even Grace, who is the person I share most things with. And definitely not Trent. Never Trent. And yet, he saw the one thing I absolutely wouldn't ever show anyone, the love letter. It was in its envelope at the bottom of the trunk for several years. I'm not even sure why I kept it.

So, Trent and I usually meet at the restaurant, but the only choices we had left for Asian at this point were dives. So we were going to meet at my house and decide which one was the least dive-iest and eat there. He showed up on time, but I wasn't ready. I wanted to take a shower. I'd overslept that morning and hadn't had time for one. I felt yucky all day.

I know I should have been ready before he arrived, but I'd been taking a leisurely stroll down memory lane. It started, as these times so often do, with a song on the radio. It was one of those that I would categorize as "our song."

Whose song you ask? Let's just say it was a high school boyfriend. I hope that will be sufficiently vague enough to keep anyone from guessing who it was. I'll call him Corey on here.

We actually had three or four songs that were "our song." I don't know if Corey realized it though. In fact, I don't know if he realized we were still dating there at the end. Or maybe we weren't, and I was the one who didn't know it. We hadn't officially broken up or had one of those "let's see other people" talks, but he'd moved away to a neighboring town senior year. I'm afraid that when he did, he moved on in other ways that I didn't know about. He'd still call me, though, and say "We ought to go out sometime." I'd agree; he wouldn't specify when, and nothing would come of it.

Well, it all went south fast one night when a friend and I ran into him at a movie. At first I was excited to see him although he seemed kind of uncomfortable. This was explained when a tall, blond girl came out of the restroom and joined him. Spindly was a good word for her. She hung on his arm; that's all I remember. I couldn't say anything and immediately left. I don't know if he tried to come after me to explain. What explanation could he give?

So, what did I do? Cried, sure, but to make matters worse, I went home and reread a card he'd written to me on my last birthday. He'd quoted what I thought was our song and talked about how much he loved me. You'd think that would be the time to tear up that card in teeny tiny bits and flush it, give it a fitting burial at sea. Dousing it with gasoline and striking a match might have been another good idea. But no. I guess I wanted to torture myself. I kept reading the stupid thing over and over, crying all the time of course.

When I couldn't cry any more, I wrote him a letter. I poured out my broken heart and tried to reassemble all of the pathetic pieces for him in the letter. What was I thinking? That he'd read it and realize that I loved him more than the blond bimbo?

Fortunately, while I was looking for a stamp I came to myself. I reread the thing and had the good sense not to send it. Why did I keep it, though? Did I need a physical reminder of how pitiful I felt? In my defense, I don't remember putting it in the trunk.

Well, when I came home tonight, with the song still playing in my head, I dragged out a necklace he'd given me, opened the chest, and reread the card. The love letter I wrote was right next to it. I was reading it when the doorbell rang. I dropped it on the bed, ran to answer the door; then I hurried into the shower so I wouldn't keep Trent waiting.

I got dressed. When I was putting on my makeup I saw the Perfect Peach lip color I'd bought from Brooke. I hadn't used it yet. I opened it and unwound it a little, but all I could see was the portrait of Trent. I put it away.

I went out to the living room, and we read some reviews online to choose which of the remaining restaurants we would favor with our business. It was hard to decide.

It was the dive-iest of dives. It smelled strongly of hot and sour soup and was completely deserted. Trent and I sat down anyway. (Remember we were on a mission.) Ignoring the smell permeating the place, we ordered won ton soup and egg rolls. The waiter left for the kitchen. I stood up, about to excuse myself to visit the ladies' room, when

Trent cleared his throat and put his hand on my arm to stop me. I sat down.

He looked a little nervous. I wondered if this was finally going to be the time he told me "the news" that I'd been dreading to hear... that he was marrying Brooke.

"Annika, there are a couple of things we need to discuss. First, I read the letter you wrote, and I think that's a big part of the reason you're having such a hard finding someone..."

Now I'm sure you're wondering why Trent was in my bedroom. I would have wondered that, too, except when he saw the look on my face, he must have assumed I was shocked at the thought that he would do that. He hurried to assure me that he'd followed me in there to ask a question. I was already in the shower by that time, and he just happened to see my letter lying on the bed...

Before I knew what I was doing, I jumped up out of my chair, knocking the tray of food out of the hands of the waiter who had just approached behind me. We were both doused with lukewarm won ton soup. Egg rolls bounced on the floor, but I barely noticed.

"Having a hard time finding someone? What do you know about it?"

"I care about you. I want you to be happy."

"I'm not holding on to some long lost love from high school!"

Trent was so calm; it was maddening. "I didn't say you were." He stood up and threw some napkins on the floor to help soak up the spreading soup broth.

"Then who cares about that stupid letter?"

"You do," he said quietly. "Or you wouldn't have kept it all these years. Why hold onto the pain?"

"I completely forgot it was in my trunk," I said.

"Then maybe you need to do some housecleaning... in more ways than one." When I didn't say anything, Trent tossed some money on the table and left.

We'd ridden together so I had to follow him out, not that I wanted to stick around. The waiter was muttering something unintelligible behind me. It didn't sound good.

When I got outside, I realized I couldn't bear to ride with him. I called a taxi and went back into the ladies room to wait for my ride. I admit I was hiding from Trent. When he saw that I wasn't coming out he left, fortunately.

I don't know how much longer I could have stood that restroom. There were crickets everywhere! Am I alone in my dread of the things? They finally drove me outside. This place wins the prize for biggest dive.

That will be in my next blog by the way, if they haven't gone out of business by the time I write it.

* * *

I woke up this morning angst-ridden, with a headache from crying, and it hit me that my "chest of remembrances" is actually a "hopeless chest." Why am I keeping mementos of relationships gone bad? Why would I keep something that made me sad to look at it? Why would I "hold onto the pain?" Was it just to remind myself that someone loved me once? Well, that's pathetic.

I pulled each item out of the trunk, stuffed them into a garbage bag and put that out with the trash. Then I went through my jewelry box and did the same thing. I'm not even giving these things away. None of it is worth anything. It's all garbage to me.

I don't have anything to put in the trunk. It'll just be empty for right now, decorated, though, with that beautiful velvet throw, so my room doesn't look any different.

Trent texted me and left phone messages. I deleted them without reading or listening to them. He's crossed a line that shouldn't be crossed. I don't ever want to see or speak to him again. I've blocked his number on my phone.

Some of you voiced the opinion that I am in love with Trent; that I'm dreading to hear of his upcoming nuptials for that reason. Wrongo readers. You need to go back farther and read my early posts. Trent was a good friend. Things change when people marry. I didn't want to lose him as a friend, although it happened anyway.

All of that angst took time and made me late for work. Angst is so draining.

There was a surprise awaiting me when I arrived this morning. Jack has resigned! I know what you're thinking; the man couldn't take dating so many women in the same office at once. (Who knows who else he was stringing along.) We weren't given an official reason, but I heard that he got a great job in another town that he just couldn't pass up. I'm certainly not heartbroken. Actually, I'm kind of relieved. Now I have a little more time to figure out what's going on with our books. There will be a hunt for his successor, of course, and that could take a while. Jack sure hasn't been here for very long. He didn't give much notice, either, just a few days; then he came down with a cold and is staying home. Sayonara, Jack old boy. Don't let the office door hit you on the way out.

I can't say I'll miss him. What I've really missed is the sugar. It's been rougher giving it up than I thought it would be. I almost caved this morning when Nadine brought in doughnuts from Elite Donuts. Suffice to say these were special ones that you don't have every day. Key lime pie, anyone? Or how about one topped with Ande's mints? Don't you hate it when you're trying to eat smart, and someone brings in long Johns painted with maple frosting and liberally sprinkled with bacon? I've always wanted to try one of those. Add the box of chocolates into the mix, and I'm absolutely surrounded by sugar. I will be strong, though.

I meet with the representative from the bank tomorrow. If I can't solve this mess with the rep I don't know what I'm going to do about the accounts. I guess I'll have to turn them over to the auditors to figure out what happened, because I'm stumped. Since this is anonymous, I can tell you it's quite a bit of money, too. Thousands. Prayer that this is just a bank error is appreciated.

I don't have any dates lined up. I think I've exhausted the list of friends and family of my friends and family.

Chapter Twenty-five

Some of you chastised me for wasting perfectly good jewelry because I tossed it instead of donating it. It's costume jewelry, people, and it was only a few items. You missed the important point here: it was a symbolic gesture that none of it is controlling my life anymore.

I didn't meet with the customer service representative from the bank today. I'm not in any shape to see people. I'm sick. On top of my cold I must have caught a stomach bug. Maybe it was something I ate. I had Mexican yesterday, so maybe it's Montezuma's Revenge. Mostly diarrhea is involved. Sorry for sharing so many details, especially if you're like me and even the thought of this stuff is making you ill.

Okay, I'll confess. I may have fallen off the diet wagon yesterday after I wrote that blog. I had a few pieces of the candy and a couple of bites of doughnut. In fact, I blame the candy for making me want the doughnuts. You know how it is, once you've blown it, you figure you might as well have everything you've been doing without since you've already ruined it for the day. I had a bite or two of the maple and bacon long John. And a little of the Key lime-filled one. They're very sweet, but the crispy bacon with the sweet of the maple was just heavenly.

All right, maybe I had more than a couple of bites. I ate almost the whole bacon long John and half of the Key lime one. When I feel up to strapping on the old feed bag again I'm off sugar. Even if the candy and doughnuts didn't cause my ailment, my mind is associating them with it, and that's enough of a connection for me. I already gave the chocolates to Nadine, kind of a peace offering for the whole Jack thing.

We had a heart to heart. We both agreed that neither of us should have dated him. She never went out with Tom Carter the fitness center guy, either. For some reason, that made me feel better. Actually, she called him and invited him out, but he graciously declined.

This post will have to be short. I think I need some more ginger ale.

* * *

It wasn't the Mexican food, so all of you people who left comments saying you have to actually visit a Latin American country to have Montezuma's Revenge wasted your time. That was a joke, anyway, folks. I'd think you'd get my sense of humor by now.

It must be a stomach bug, because most of the people in my office caught it. Nadine and Zoe ended up dehydrated, with Nadine going to the

ER for an IV.

I'm still not better either, but I think the ginger ale kept me hydrated enough to avoid the ER. I'm going back to bed.

* * *

I made two discoveries today. It wasn't stomach flu that we all had. It was the chocolate! I don't know how, but someone must have put something in the box of chocolates to make us sick. Since they're from Jack, he's the likely culprit, of course... especially in light of the other discovery I made.

Since I was able to return to work today, I also met with someone from customer service at the bank. We finally figured out what happened to the missing money. Jack must have taken it! He absconded with our funds, and must have laced my chocolate to make me sick enough to keep me from finding out about his theft! Unfortunately, after Nadine ate half the box, she shared the candy with everyone in the office. Don't write and rag on poor Nadine because of her lack of self-control. Trust me; she's suffered enough. We're turning the few remaining pieces of candy over to the police.

I found out that somehow when Jack solicited funds for the

organization, the check was written out to him instead of to our non-profit. Then he must have cashed the check through his own personal account. The only reason he got caught at all, is because the couple who donated the money later submitted a form for a receipt for tax purposes, so I recorded it as received then, but the money was never deposited into our account.

A couple of thoughts have occurred to me. First, I think Jack was only paying attention to me to keep me distracted from my work. Second, I'm assuming he thought any blame for the missing money would fall on me. Worst. Boss. Ever!

The police are looking for him. It turns out he was using an alias, and of course the story he told us about moving to that nearby town was false. If he'd been the one to issue the tax receipt, it wouldn't have been recorded at all, so who knows how many times he's done this, how much he took. It's a good thing he wasn't here very long.

A couple of thoughts have occurred to me. First, I think Jack was only paying attention to me to keep me distracted from my work. Second, I'm assuming he thought any blame for the missing money would fall on me. Worst. Boss. Ever!

* * *

The police reported back from the lab. There was Ex-lax in the chocolates. Turns out I was wrong to suspect that Jack gave me the tainted candy, though. I'd forgotten he ate a couple of them himself. He went home sick that day. I thought he left because of his cold, but Zoe told me today he left because he had what we had. Since Jack didn't mess with the chocolate, that must mean I still have Hunter stalking me.

I also remembered Jack's confusion when I broke things off with him. He'd seemed genuinely puzzled when I talked about the box of chocolates, so that first box of candy must not have been from him, either. No one got sick from those chocolates, of course. Now the police are going to question Hunter.

* * *

Brand new twist! The police are convinced that Hunter is not the one stalking me. Other than murdering the stuffed dog that first night, he may not have done any of the other stalkerish stuff. Zoe was questioned by the police and not only was the guy who delivered the candy the same person both times, but he had blond hair. Hunter has dark brown hair. Before you write and ask me if I've ever heard of the concept of a wig or hair dye, the police showed her a picture, and she said it wasn't him. The police tried to bring Hunter in for questioning, and it turns out he'd taken a different job several states away some time ago. Now they think the stalker must have been someone else all along... someone that I've dated!

The first person I thought of was Geoff. The guy plays war games on a date, and he does have blond hair. He's so sweet though. I can't see him doing all of that mean stuff, and he never seemed mad that I wasn't interested in dating him.

I finally decided Dylan was the most likely with his disturbing ideas about dating, but it doesn't seem fair to single him out either. The police told me that messing with the chocolates like that is a felony! I certainly don't want to falsely accuse someone. I just have no idea.

When I thought I knew who the stalker was, believe it or not, it was comforting, even though he wouldn't stop bothering me. Not knowing is frightening. I'm constantly surveying my surroundings on my drive to work, looking for him... whoever he is. Grace and I moved back in with our parents again. I'm on edge all of the time.

The police want a list of guys I've dated that the stalker could be. What was I thinking to go out with all of those men? I'm embarrassed to give all of their names to the police. You can imagine what they'll think of me! I have no idea where most of them live. There were so many, I don't think I can even remember what they did for a living. I mean I have this blog, of course, but I changed so many of the details that it's kind of a big blur. I have to come up with the list by tomorrow.

* * *

Yes, it was embarrassing giving the list to the police. One of them raised his eyebrows and took another sidelong glance at me. I rushed out an explanation of my blind date experiment. He nodded, but from the looks passing between the two officers, I wonder if they were satisfied with my response. I'm sure they had quite a discussion about me in the squad car later.

I've got another date lined up tonight. I'm sure you're wondering why I'm willing to go out with someone... anyone, after all I've been through with this stalker. Well, this is another guy my dad knows, Melvin, so he's safe. I'll let you know what happens. I can predict Melvin even before I meet him. He'll be a little older than I am (or a lot older). I think Dad sees them as more stable. I guess that's true in a way. He'll be a bit of a nerd or very much so. Maybe Dad thinks that's the best I can do. I blame Tilly for planting that thought in his brain. Or maybe it's only in my brain.

Dad's Aunt Tilly was sitting with us at one of my siblings' wedding reception. I've forgotten which one. I was about eleven, so Grace was nine. We were all eating wedding cake, having a good time. Cake was my favorite part of every wedding.

Aunt Tilly had to do the thing that great aunts seem to gravitate toward at some point during visits: comparing the siblings. She went down the line making predictions, dire and otherwise about all of us. (She hit the nail on the head with John who holds the world record for most jobs.) Mom and Dad are always very patient with Tilly, whose filter broke down about twenty-five years ago. When she reached Grace and me, I think she forgot we were actually sitting there. She said "Grace and Annika look a lot alike except Grace is the pretty one." Yes, she did say that. Then she seemed to notice me. Maybe because my mouth fell open. Anyway, to recover, she said, "Grace isn't that much prettier, she's just more petite. You must be careful with the sweets, dear, or you'll never catch a man." Even at eleven I knew she meant I was a cow. I had to walk away from the cake that day, couldn't take another bite. She ruined wedding cake for me. Every time I taste one, I remember that day.

Chapter Twenty-six

My date last night was not significant, but what happened on it was. We ran into Grace. Yeah, she was so not out with friends all of those times. Who was she dating? You'll never guess... Tom Carter, the fitness guy!

Let me tell you, I was shocked. Melvin and I ended up seated next to their table. When I saw them, I went right over and insisted, I mean invited them to join us. Grace was squirming, looking like she was trying to figure out a way to refuse, but Tom immediately got up and moved their plates over to our table, letting their waiter know they would finish their meal with us.

You may remember that Grace knew Tom from college. When I mentioned him to her back when Nadine and I went shopping for juicy guys at the fitness center, Grace just happened to wander in off the street a few days later. She pulled that same gag about considering membership, wandering around the fitness center with him until the idea hit him to ask her out. It sounds like it took nearly two hours. He's not the brightest bulb in the package.

I can't believe my little sister has been hiding this from me all this time. Tom is not for Grace. She wouldn't be happy with him. Sure, he's good-looking and fit, but that's probably the problem. The man is too self-absorbed for Grace. And he's a player!

After we got home, we had quite a few words, mostly about deceiving her sister and roommate about what she has been doing all along. So how does she defend herself? You will not believe it. She blamed it on me! Grace had the nerve to say that I am the one who is self-absorbed, and if I'd been paying better attention I would have known that she was dating someone. Of course I set her straight. Other than the dates, which take a lot of my time, I have had a stalker and trouble at work. Self-absorbed? I have to be for my own survival. And why should I have to figure it out on my own, anyway?

Now guess the reason she said she didn't tell me that the name of the person she was dating was Tom. You never will. She said that I am just too picky about men! Can you believe she said that? She said I wouldn't have approved of him no matter who he was. She pointed out that she was right because I don't approve of him. Of course I don't. He's all wrong for her.

So then she had the gall to say that she knows better than I do who is right for me. Okay, am I the only person who sees that she is a hypocrite? She said several of the dates should have gone on to second dates, but that I didn't let them. When I brought up Ben, she said he didn't count because I'd already dated him, and that he didn't last long either.

She's convinced that I don't know a good thing when I find it. She even said she knew who was Mr. Right (for me) but I'm too dense to recognize it. She won't give me a name. Whatever. None of them were right for me. She's just saying that to get back at me.

Or maybe she's not. Some of you have been here all along. So I put two questions to you. Am I self-absorbed, and who is the guy Grace is so certain is the man for me? I'll tell you; it wasn't Melvin. He almost made Tom look good!

* * *

Kidding, people! Melvin didn't improve my opinion of Tom. And I didn't mean Mel was insignificant as a person, just as a date. A lot of you wanted to know what was wrong with Mel. I assumed you wouldn't need me to describe the guy. I named him Melvin. What else did you need to know? If you are still so unimaginative then, fine, I'll describe him: quiet, blinks a lot, a little distant. For those of you who need a physical description: dark, unruly hair, glasses. He's very smart, probably a professor. I think those are the only guys my dad knows. I don't think we ever got around to discussing his occupation.

Most of you voted for Geoff as the mystery man Grace is referring to. A few said Trent in spite of the fact that I have told you all along that he is a friend. I'm not sure why you maintain this, like dating a guy who's been a friend for years is romantic. Hmm, totally not romantic, people. Anyway, even if he hadn't been dating someone for a long time, I haven't talked to him in I don't know how long and have no plans to do so. Ever.

At any rate, since the Ex-lax incident, the stalker hasn't sent any more, um, presents. I know this sounds paranoid, but I suspect someone's watching me. I haven't seen anyone. It's more of a feeling I get.

* * *

Someone pointed out that I named Melvin before I met him. Sure I did. I knew what kind of person my dad would fix me up with. No need to change his name after I met him. It fit.

So you're wondering if I knew, why didn't I skip the date? I just couldn't take a chance. You never know when Mr. Right will suddenly appear before you. It's like how it is with fortune cookies. I don't really believe in them, but if a fortune cookie confirms what I was already thinking... well couldn't the same thing happen in life? One of these times,

Dad might pull it off: a magic rabbit out of a hat instead of a nerd. Either way, the guy he'll pick is safe.

I have not been successful in talking Grace out of dating Tom. Tonight the family meets him for the first time. I will try to restrict my gloating, but I'm sure they won't like him any more than I do.

* * *

Well, the clan met, and the jury's still out on what the family thinks of Tom. My parents were okay with him. Most of my siblings didn't have an opinion one way or another. Well, maybe if they saw him walking around flirting with a complete stranger, like Tom did with Nadine, they might not think so well of him. The guy's a player!

I can't tell you how many texts and voicemail messages have been left on my phone by the "ex-blind dates." Um, most of them basically hate me, now. Seems having the police contact you as a possible stalker leaves a bad taste in the mouth. I do regret causing them this trouble. None of them were meant to be, though, so it's not catastrophic.

Geoff and Ben actually both left messages expressing how sorry they were that I was going through such a scary time, and that they'd like to give our relationship another try. Geoff was nice about it. I might consider a date with him, but no way would I want to go out with Ben

again. I'm not even answering his voicemail. He may have put me off

hamburgers for life!

* * *

I texted Geoff back that I'd like to talk to him, and he called me.

We had a nice conversation and a good laugh about the paintball date. It

turns out he wasn't the one who kept exploding the paint grenades over my

hiding place that day. It must have been that punk kid who had it out for

me. I've always suspected him.

We met at Nunzio's for Italian tonight. I'll admit with all of this

stalker business I wasn't comfortable giving out my address. The police

are still looking for the guy, you know. Geoff thinks it's terrible that

someone would do that. He seems sincere. Still, better to be safe, so I

suggested meeting at the restaurant.

I haven't been here since I had lunch with Jack. The police are still

looking for him, too. Funny how the police are on a manhunt for two

people that I've known/dated. The police never were involved in my life

before except for the occasional stray traffic ticket. I miss those days.

Anyway, back to my date. Nunzio's was just as good as I

remember it. I had ravioli. (They have the best in town). I haven't been out in quite a while (for me) except for Melvin, and I couldn't even tell you what I ate that night; I was so upset with Grace for the whole dating Tom on the sly thing. Geoff and I had a very nice time. We talked about family and work. He's a mechanic. I admire a man who can work with his hands. I obviously can't.

After supper Geoff suggested a walk by the river rather than going to a movie, play, or paintball. Our town has a lighted path. There were a lot of couples and families walking along there. Isn't it better to do something like that rather than go to a movie, where the focus is on the screen, and you can't talk? You already know where I stand on Annika not talking. The focus on our date last night was to get to know each other better. There wasn't a lot of talking on our other date when we were trying to annihilate each other with paint.

He asked me out again for tomorrow night, so not only has a blind date finally gone on to a second, but now even a third. Things are looking up!

* * *

I've decided Crazycatlady needs a hobby. Something offline. She said that I'm only going out with Geoff again because Grace said that none of my blind dates went on to second dates. That's not why I went out again.

I decided I was wrong about Geoff. I got to know him better when we met in the coffee shop by accident (twice), and he stood up to Ben for me when Ben was being pushy. It's a nice trait that he defends people he thinks are in trouble, and honestly he's quite brave. Ben is a big guy. Geoff even offered me a ride home that night. We might have gone out again back then, except he could see I was dating Ben at the time.

We had fun on our date last night. It just goes to show you that you should always give people a second chance, although to be honest, there isn't another blind date I'm willing to try again.

Geoff wants to surprise me tonight, so I don't know where we're going.

* * *

We went to the Japanese Tranquil Garden. Our town has a park set up as a JTG. Kind of surprising, since there isn't a large Japanese population here. It was nice, peaceful, very Zen. The perfect place to break up with someone. I'd suggest JTG to all of you out there if you're in the mood to cut someone loose. People are probably less likely to make a scene in a setting like that. I should have told Ben sayonara there.

Yeah, I wasn't just tossing that out there. Geoff and I ended our dating relationship. We've had only three dates, or really two and a half dates, since this one ended shortly after we arrived, so I don't know if you can exactly say we broke up. We didn't have anything solid to sever.

It didn't break my heart, either, but it was kind of sad. I liked Geoff a lot. I'm glad it ended before it went any further, though.

We walked in and immediately went to the tea ceremony they were having. More calming Zen-like stuff. Except for two cute little Japanese kids, a boy and a girl, who were making a lot of noise in the corner. They were just darling! I wanted to scoop them up and take them home, except that's illegal. Or better, offer to babysit while their parents went out. I guess they might think that's odd, a stranger coming up out of the blue like that. I'm sure they would have hurried their children away from me, maybe called the police. They were just so stinking cute!

Geoff didn't think so. I mean, he didn't exactly say that, but when the ceremony was over, he mentioned that the kids ruined it! I was sure he and I weren't talking about the same kids, but yep, we were. Turns out he isn't that in to children, having a family, stuff like that. I always supposed there were men out there like that, but they hadn't revealed it to me.

Maybe because that's not something you talk about on a first date.

Geoff must have had a troubled childhood. He intimated that. Not only does he not see himself as ever being a father, but he sees kids as little more than a nuisance, a necessary evil to repopulate the earth. He wasn't that mean about it; those weren't his exact words, but that's what he meant.

I immediately told him that's the opposite of how I feel. Obviously that's a deal breaker for me. We were both nice about it, of course, but I'm passionate about someday having a family. He left.

I stayed and wandered around the garden, went down to the pond and watched the lily pads floating. It's still peaceful, but not much fun to be there alone. Like everything else in life.

A family came along, the parents walking hand in hand, with two small tow-headed children running ahead, racing each other to a footbridge. The little boy won, and danced around like it was the biggest thing he'd ever done in life. Maybe it was. I teared up. Was I ever going to have a moment like that with my own family?

Chapter Twenty-seven

It's been a few days since I've posted. I didn't have anything newsworthy to say, not that that's ever stopped me before, but I do now. I never thought it would happen this way, but my baby sister is making the biggest mistake of her life. Grace and Tom are engaged! They popped it on everyone last night when we got together for pizza after my niece's soccer game. Is that an appropriate venue to announce an engagement? When everyone is sweaty and dressed in jeans and T-shirts? Not to mention the obvious. It's too soon. They haven't known each other long enough for this step. Grace insists it's been a long time. Actually, it's been as long as I've been writing this blog... so just a few months. She also pointed out that they're not getting married yet. They're only engaged. I still say it's too soon.

And what did she do right away? She set up an appointment to go shopping for the dress with all of the women in the family. It's practically a party. It's tonight for goodness sake! I don't know if I'm going. What's there to celebrate? Grace marrying the wrong guy? I'm sure many of my longtime readers will agree with me here. It's all very depressing.

And who does that... shops for a dress the day after she announces their engagement, when they haven't even set the date? It's like the romance of a wedding is what she's in love with, not Tom.

They don't still ask that question during the ceremony about if anyone objects to the wedding, do they? I think they should keep that in there.

* * *

Ben is making a nuisance of himself. He's called several times, left voicemail messages, and texted me. Yeah, not going out again with Burger Guy ever.

Again, I was kidding on my last post, people! I wouldn't object at my sister's wedding like that, even though I'm objecting constantly right up to the minute she walks down the aisle. Several of you weighed in on that last blog exceptionally fast, saying you think I'm jealous! I am not interested in Tom Carter of all people.

Many also mentioned that I was being petty, and that neither Grace nor I would ever forgive me if I wasn't there tonight at her dress tryon. Don't worry; I'm going. It's bad enough she's got the wrong groom. I don't want her to buy the wrong dress, too.

* * *

Dress shopping either went well or was totally catastrophic depending on whether you're Grace or me. Grace fell in love with the first dress she found (not unlike her experience with Tom), but she also tried on a couple of other gowns to humor the family because they didn't want her to buy the first one she saw. The woman helping her at the shop said it often happens that way. (With the dress, not with the guy; we didn't ask her opinion on that.)

At first it was okay. I teared up when Grace emerged from the dressing room, for the right reason. She looked beautiful and was the epitome of her name, which is why I chose it for her on here.

Unfortunately, the tears wouldn't stop. Pretty soon it was getting embarrassing. Then my oldest sister, Ruth, did the worst thing she could do, she offered sympathy. She put an arm around my shoulder and said "Everything will be all right, Annika. Your turn will come."

Well, then I definitely couldn't stop crying. I knew my turn wouldn't come. She was just saying that to make me feel better. To make matters worse, I tried to explain that my tears were because it was so touching to see Grace in her wedding dress, which was true in the beginning. But by then it was turning into sobbing and hiccupping.

Sentences weren't being finished. No one was buying it.

Neither was I. All of the months of blind dating, not to mention the years of waiting for Mr. Right, and I was no closer to buying my own wedding dress than I had been months ago when I started this whole crazy thing. I had been counting on this experiment to finally find the man of my dreams and fall in love.

Tom's mother and sister looked at each other like "What kind of weirdo family is Tom marrying into?" It was bad enough to lose it in front of my family, but to go to pieces in front of strangers was too much.

I ran out to my car. I couldn't see to drive, so I pulled into a nearby Dairy Queen until I could stop crying. Maybe with the unhinged sister gone, the rest of them could explain my behavior by saying that becoming an old maid had hit me hard.

That's what I'm going to be. It might be politically incorrect to use that term these days, but I might as well face it. No one wants me, and I'm going to spend my life alone.

* * *

Yes, I had some ice cream while I was at Dairy Queen, a root beer float. You know me very well. Ice cream is very comforting.

Your encouragement is appreciated. And you're right; life isn't over because my younger sister is getting married, and I'm not.

I just wish Grace had picked someone I could be happy for her about. Marriage is one of the biggest steps she'll take in this life. I love my little sister; I don't want her to marry the wrong guy.

I'm ready to pronounce this experiment a failure. I didn't date anyone I was really interested in. I certainly didn't find the love of my life. I'd always dreaded the thought of being a spinster. I don't welcome it now, but there are other things in life. Maybe I'll get a cat.

I started thinking about the last date someone arranged for me... Melvin. The only reason I was willing to go out with him was because he was safe. So what was I going to do... automatically exclude anyone who would have given me a real shot at happiness, because I was scared of a stalker? But I was afraid of more than that.

What if I mess this up? In spite of the fact that I've made fun on here of most of the dates, and seem to be taking the whole thing lightly, marriage is a serious step to me. I don't want some psycho, lunatic killer, but I also don't want to settle for someone just because he's safe. I want to be madly, completely, hopelessly in love. I want someone that I can not only live with, but also someone I can't live without.

I'm convinced a lot of women feel they can't live without the guy they're dating because they move too fast in the relationship. That's one of the reasons sex before marriage is a bad idea. It's investing yourself totally in something that neither of you has committed to, a lifelong relationship. Can you think rationally after giving yourself to someone in that way? Above all else, clear heads are called for in a dating relationship.

Grace and Tom have set the date, by the way. They're out right now choosing a photographer. They're inseparable most of the time anyway. I'm still not happy about her choice of men, but I'm resigned.

The police haven't solved the mystery of who my stalker is. He hasn't contacted me lately, but the guy should be found and charged with the food tampering crime, anyway. I still have an unsettled feeling not knowing who it is. Maybe that's why I feel like someone is watching me all the time.

I'll keep posting on here, at least a few more entries to wrap things up about Grace. Maybe I'll do my other blog after that; the one about the Asian restaurants. I'm about to have a lot of free time.

* * *

Thank you for the outpouring of sympathy, and also for those of you who refuse to let me feel sorry for myself. You're right. Even though I didn't find a guy, I have a great job and a wonderful family. I did lose one of my best friends, but I guess I've accepted that. I'm going to focus on what is good.

I stopped to drop something off for Grace's wedding at my parents' house on the way to work this morning. Mom had made coffee cake, so I had a piece and a cup of coffee. Mom gave me a hug and asked what's been bothering me.

Where do I start, Mom? I didn't have time for this, nor did I want to go into work with a headache from crying, so I just shrugged and said "nothing really, Mom." I focused on finishing the cake.

"I've know a lot of women older than you when they got married. Thirty is not old. Don't give up, Annika."

"I just don't want to end up like Miss Martha, Mom," I said.

"Sometimes women end up widowed. You can't help that kind of thing," she said, putting another piece of coffee cake on my plate.

"Widowed? I thought she was an old maid! Her name was Miss Martha."

"Calling ladies Miss and their first name is just a courteous way of addressing women in the South. She married but was widowed early, and her only son lived in another state. He didn't visit much. "

For some reason, that didn't make me feel much better. I could think of other examples of old maids after all.

"Miss Martha notwithstanding, I don't want to end up alone, Mom."

My normally sympathetic mom just said, "There are worse things in life."

Well, yeah. I could fall from a twenty-story building, Mom. Not sure where she was going with that.

After I got to work, I noticed a coworker, Gillian, looked like she'd been crying. Zoe had the scoop.

"Marriage troubles," she whispered when she saw me looking at Gillian.

"Oh, I wasn't trying to pry."

"I overheard her say her husband hasn't been home before midnight for a month," she said.

Zoe is the worst gossip, or actually, maybe she's the best, if you think about the meaning of the word. Either way, I didn't need to hear what she overheard. I went to the break room and got a cup of coffee. On my way back to my desk I saw that Gillian still looked very unhappy.

I knew that basically Mom meant "Stop feeling sorry for yourself, Annika." After all, you can always find someone better off or worse than you if you paid attention. More than comparing my circumstances to other people, though, maybe I need to get outside of myself. Just brighten the corner where I am, so to speak.

When I went out for lunch, I picked up a couple of small bunches of flowers from the grocery story. One bouquet went in my office right on the corner of my desk where I could see it every time I glanced up. The other bouquet I left in Gillian's office with a note of encouragement.

She came in later to thank me for them. She noticed my matching bouquet.

"I think we all could use something to perk up our offices and our lives," I said.

She shut the door and confided in me that she'd made the decision to leave her husband. And it had been only a week, not a month that he'd been coming home late, as Zoe had said. Just goes to show you shouldn't believe the gossip you hear.

I hadn't meant to force a confidence from her, but since she felt comfortable sharing with me, I let her know I was available if she needed to talk. I'm sure there's no advice I could give her since I've never been married, but everyone needs a sympathetic ear some time. I asked her if I could pray for her. She was open to it, so I prayed a quick prayer that God's will would be done in her life.

I know it wasn't a monumental thing to do, offering a prayer and a small bunch of flowers to a coworker, but just knowing someone cares can make a big difference.

You know that saying "Time and tide wait for no man"? I'm sure it's supposed to be about wasted opportunities that once are lost can't be regained. Something else struck me when I heard it today.

Try to stop time. Try to stop a tide. You have no control over either. You always hear people saying "You can do anything you put your mind to." Um, no. No you can't. You can go with the flow, though, rather than fight the tide, and just focus on the things you can do something about, even if it isn't monumental. So Grace and I are going to try to help the world be a better place even though it's just one small thing. We're going to go to the shelter and rescue an animal that needs us.

Chapter Twenty-eight

Grace and I have rescued a white cat. His name is either Lamb if you're Grace or Lam if you're me, so there is something new in my life to love, at least theoretically. I wanted a dog, but with us being gone all day, we settled on a cat.

It's hard to fall in love with a cat. They're more autonomous. This one is particularly so, and is rarely seen, hence my take on the name. He's slightly psychotic, too, so he fits right into our home. Half the time, I'm sure he must have committed a crime and taken it on the lam. The rest of the time he either perches on places we can't reach, or if he is feeling particularly brave, he parks himself behind us on the top of the couch or chair and flicks his tail under our noses. If you try to swat at it he spits and hisses and refuses to stop. Then if we can capture him and put him in the laundry room, he yowls.

I've decided Lam would make a nice housewarming gift for Grace and Tom after they get married. Maybe he could just be waiting for them in their new home after they return from their honeymoon. Wouldn't that be a nice surprise?

I think I'll visit one of those Asian dives tonight to finish the list of restaurants for my next blog. It's the last one on my list since several have closed since Trent and I began our experiment. Never thought I'd end up being an online food critic, but that's the new blog in the works.

I hate eating in restaurants alone. I'd get it to go, but that would defeat the purpose of the visit. I guess I could invite Nadine or someone, but it doesn't seem right to do this with anyone but Trent.

Speaking of Trent, something happened a few months ago that I didn't tell the whole story about. No, I'll admit that I didn't forget this detail. I left it out purposely. I don't know why.

I was out on a date with someone, I forget who now. We went to a movie and while we were waiting in line, I saw Trent up ahead with Brooke. They were standing in line, holding hands, and they kissed. That's the part I didn't mention. Forget about your views on PDA, I'd never seen them kiss before. I'll admit that it shocked me. In fact, that's the real reason we hadn't gone out for Chinese in so long. I just thought it would feel weird to see him after that.

As you know, the last time he and I got together, he let me know he had a couple of things to say. I thought at the time that he was going to spring their engagement on me. That was probably the other thing he had to tell me, but I ran out of the restaurant so fast after his confession of reading the love letter, and then I was so upset, he didn't get a chance to tell me. Of course I've blocked him since then.

He's been such a constant in my life for years. I can't believe he's gone. I guess I knew it was bound to happen anyway, when he and Brooke got close. But that day was always some time in the distant future. It wasn't in the now. Between my sister's impending wedding, the stalker, and this, my life has become something I don't recognize.

* * *

So guess who showed up tonight at the restaurant! Trent! Grace must have told him I'd be there.

He walked right in, pulled up a chair, and planted himself like he'd never done what he did. Like our friendship hadn't ended. I guess he doesn't realize that some things that are lost are lost forever.

I refused to talk to him, of course. I made the fastest exit you've ever seen. He tried to follow me. I just can't face him, and I can't forgive him, so why talk?

I drove around for a little while; then I went back and got an order to go so I can review it for my Asian food blog. Now I can say I've visited every one of these restaurants in our city. It might not seem like much to you, but I consider it quite an accomplishment. I ate at fifty restaurants give or take a few, and took notes on every visit.

I've had to block Ben. He's been texting me and calling me ever since the police contacted him. Jason sent me a nice little text telling me exactly what he thought of me. He has quite a vocabulary, that one. I've decided Zoe is not a very good judge of character. At least not in the man department.

On a happier note, I've lost a total of ten pounds skipping sugar and other junk. Well, skipping it most of the time. I took up jogging, too. Well, walking and jogging. Okay, I walk, but pretty soon I'm going to start the jogging part of my workout. I'm doing the Couch to 5K. Actually, I'm doing a modified version of it. At least I'm off the couch. That's a start!

* * *

Annikawhatareyouthinking is convinced that Trent is in love with me, especially after last night. Have you been keeping up with my posts? Go back and catch up before you comment again.

I bought an exercise bike and gave up on the walking/jogging thing. I keep feeling like someone is following me. Maybe it's my imagination because of the stalker, but the feeling was disturbing enough to chase me indoors. Besides, I can watch TV or read while I exercise, so I'm multi-tasking. It makes me feel efficient.

The board has finally replaced Jack. The police never found him, either. Maybe they need to hire some new detectives, since they are mystified by my stalker, too.

Anyway, this manager is older, at least twenty-five years older than I am with framed pictures of his family on his desk. It doesn't matter, since I'm never going out with anyone from work ever again. Ever.

Speaking of work, Nadine has been seeing someone, and it looks serious for once. She met him on at an online dating site, and now she is pushing for me to register on there.

Good for her, but after all of the blind dates and the stalker, I definitely don't want to go that route. I don't know why, but somehow it seems frightening now to put myself online and let guys look me over like meat in a butcher case to see if they feel like dating me.

The wedding is fast approaching with the rehearsal in a few days. I'd better end this blog; I need to put some more miles on the bike. My bridesmaid's dress was just a touch on the tight side when I bought it.

* * *

Wedding arrangements are in full swing. Grace is going around like a zombie most of the time, mumbling about whatever is on her to-do list that day in kind of a disjointed way that makes it sound like she's losing her mind. "Roses fan tuxedo bites." I'm trying to help whenever I can, so I know this translates to "Order the roses and the fans for the bridesmaids' bouquets. Did the guys get fitted for their tuxedos, yet? What does Mom think of having cheesecake bites?" She's always been on the absent-minded side as a matter of course, so it's expected that she will be even more so now.

Tom is still not growing on me. He suggested setting me up with his brother. In a way, it's kind of nice of him to offer it when he knows I don't like him. On the other hand, why is he offering that when he knows I don't like him? Why would I date an older, paunchy, divorced, father of three extremely bratty kids, version of Tom? I guess you can tell I've met his brother. I'm not bothering to make up a name for the guy.

Anyway, my answer would have been no thanks, even if I hadn't already met him. I'm not interested in going on any more blind dates. Ever.

Gillian came in to talk to me again this morning. She left her husband. He had been seeing another woman. She's seems at peace with her decision. We went out for lunch, and she told me all about it. She's seeing a lawyer after work today.

I need to make this short. I'm going out for a run/jog/walk... whatever I can keep up until I collapse. The bridesmaid's dress still doesn't quite fit. It's kind of a slinky affair, and I don't want a pooching tummy ruining the effect.

Chapter Twenty-nine

I wasn't imagining it; I was being followed! I'll tell you the whole story.

I was at a park downtown exercising. I started out running, which turned into jogging after about a block, which morphed into eventually dropping in a heap. In case you're wondering, this is not the actual Couch to 5K method. This is the Annika is totally out of shape but has to fit in a tight dress that is way too small for her in less than a week method. If you're interested in my version, the next step is hanging out in the ER to expose myself to some kind of a stomach bug. Either I'll be too sick to attend the wedding, or well, you can figure out the rest of it on your own.

Anyway, I was almost back to my car when I passed the point of exhaustion part of my run and just dropped down on the grass. There was a wooden bench in another twenty feet, and my car about another twenty feet beyond that, but when I need to collapse, I like to do so immediately. I was more or less prostrate on the grass, so I got a good look, unintended though it was, behind some bushes. Trent was crouching there!

I shrieked! I was utterly shocked and started spluttering. It came out kind of like, "You! But! You! Wait! What? You?" Trent was holding up his hands as if to defend himself from the verbal and/or physical assault that he knew was coming (and deserved) once my brain started working normally again. It probably wasn't getting enough oxygen from all that running.

He said, "I was worried about you being stalked, Annika." I guess he doesn't realize that stalking someone to protect her from stalking is still stalking. I mean, he knows it now, because I shouted it over my shoulder as I took off running. My exhaustion forgotten, I had a sudden, uncharacteristic burst of energy and did the forty feet in four seconds flat. I think that must be some kind of record for slightly plump desk jockeys. I'll check the Guinness site after I get off here.

All of this exercising has made me more coordinated, and I can operate the button on my remote to unlock my car now while I'm running. I jumped in, threw that puppy in gear, and roared out of there with Trent close behind.

I'm not sure what I was doing. He knows where I live, of course. All I could think of was that I had to get away from him. Anyway, I thought I'd lost him when he had to stop at a red light, that I, um, didn't notice, but since I wasn't sure if I'd shaken him, I continued on into kind of a bad part of town.

It was getting quite dark, too, by then. Well, I got lost, tried to be clever, and went down an alley that dead-ended. When I went to back up, I found there was another car behind me. I waited a few seconds for them to notice my backup lights. They didn't move. I lightly beeped the horn. They still didn't move. I was pretty sure it wasn't Trent's car, and was considering calling 9-1-1 when someone got out and walked toward my driver's side door. I immediately locked the doors, prayed like crazy, and got out my phone.

A man bent over to look in the window. It was Ben! Relief was quickly replaced with fear when I realized he must have been following me, too. Normally, I would at least crack a window for someone I know, but intuition told me not to. Ben knocked on the window; then he angrily pounded on it. Even though he saw me calling 9-1-1 he didn't stop hitting the window. He looked around and found a big stick about the size of a baseball bat to use.

I scrambled into the back seat while I frantically told the dispatcher that I had no idea where I was. Don't these things have a GPS? I was listing the last streets I'd recognized when Ben gave up on the stick and picked up a jagged rock and started in with that. I squeezed myself into the backseat floor. It didn't take long for the rock to be effective. He must have realized he'd been hitting the strongest section of the window before and moved to the edge to find the weak part.

Crash! He smashed the window. Pieces flew everywhere. Some landed on me.

Ben has always reminded me of a bear. In the past it was a sweet teddy bear, but now, he's just a grizzly. He brushed the glass off the door and pawed around until he found the button to unlock the doors.

By this point, I was screaming into the phone for help. He yanked open the back door. I got up on the seat and started kicking at him. He was managing to avoid the maelstrom that was my flailing legs and was reaching for me when someone hit him on the back of his knees with that bat-like stick. The rescuer got in another blow on the side of the head when Ben backed out of the car. Ben went down, but his head must be made of lead, because he jumped right back up again, belying that "The bigger they are, the harder they fall" axiom.

Ben then proceeded to head-butt my rescuer, who ended up lying dazed next to a brick wall. Ben was coming for me again when I heard sirens. He ran for his car, but my rescuer had somehow managed to pull himself up off the ground and beat Ben to his own car, locking the doors behind him. Ben took off down the alley the way we'd come. Two police cars raced into the space, cutting him off. He immediately put his hands in the air before the police even told him to. He's a chicken, but a very smart chicken.

To say I was shaking like a leaf is no comparison. Are these leaves in the middle of a tornado? Otherwise I had leaves everywhere beat hands down. I couldn't talk either.

After the police cuffed Ben and shoved him none too gently into the back of the cruiser, I crept out of my car. My rescuer appeared then, too. It was Trent! Even though I'd left him behind at that stoplight, he hadn't given up trying to find me, since he'd noticed Ben was following me.

Trent was driving up and down every street when he heard me screaming. He abandoned his car in the road and was running around on foot trying to locate me. The police came upon his car in the middle of the street and found us right after that, no doubt due to my hysterical screaming. That's usually a tipoff.

When the ambulance came, I didn't need medical assistance since the glass had landed on me so softly, but Trent had hit the brick wall with the back of his head. He refused a ride to the hospital, so the EMTs just cleaned his wound and put a bandage on his head.

So, Ben was the stalker after all. I suppose in retrospect I should have guessed, since he never accepted it when I broke up with him. That had happened right before my date with Hunter, so it was actually Ben, when I thought Hunter was doing all of those stalker-ish things.

I can't tell you what a relief it is to finally have it behind me. I felt so free watching him ride off into the night with the police. The food tampering he did is a felony, and going after Trent and me the way he did won't help his case any. He should be put away for a while.

Trent didn't say much. I think getting beat up by Ben took a lot out of him. I insisted on following his car in mine to make sure he made it home okay since he refused to go to the hospital. He was exhausted. He said he'd see me tomorrow and went inside.

Tomorrow! I'd forgotten that tomorrow is the rehearsal for the wedding! I'm exhausted, too. When will the drama finally end?

* * *

Not only was Ben stalking me, but he's done this before! After he was hauled down to the police station, his fingerprints were run through the database. They discovered he's wanted for stalking some poor woman in California. In fact, I think I read about it when it happened... right before he moved back here. He was going under a different name out there. He almost killed her! I hope the guy spends his days safely tucked away in some prison. Honestly, if they have hamburgers and violent movies in the slammer, he should fit right in, anyway. Hasta la vista, baby.

275

Gillian saw a lawyer and her husband was served with papers. I guess it woke him up to what he was losing. He wants to try again. Gillian said she was willing to give him one chance if counseling is part of the agreement. I don't know if they'll make it; it's a long shot after a betrayal like that. Either way, there's a long road back to trust that they'll have to walk.

Tonight is the rehearsal. The wedding is tomorrow. Our family is meeting to decorate the church this afternoon. This has been such an emotional time for me with the stalker and all. I think Grace would have understood if I begged off, but I couldn't miss it. You can't just skip the important things in life, even if they're hard. Maybe because they're hard.

Did I tell you that Trent is a groomsman, and he's walking me down the aisle? When he said that he'd see me the next day, he meant it. Grace didn't drop the bomb on me that Trent is in the wedding until today. They barely know him! Why is he in the wedding? She mumbled something about not having enough guys for girls or something. Grace is so vague nowadays; I didn't push it.

But I did wonder why he had to walk with me, though. She just sighed and scrunched her eyes up like she was going to cry, so I didn't say anything else. I think she's on the verge of pulling me out of the wedding anyway, since I don't like Tom. You might be thinking that's what I hope she'll do, but a sister's wedding is bigger than petty squabbles. Neither of us would ever forget it if I wasn't involved on her special day, in spite of the fact that Tom will be there too.

But the important thing is that Trent is coming to the rehearsal and to the dinner afterward. He'll also be at the wedding obviously. That's three more times in my life I'll have to see him. Of course I'm grateful to him for rescuing me, although I'm kind of confused how he even knew about all of that, but the point is we've gone too far down different paths to ever go down the same one again.   I'll let you know how it goes.

Chapter Thirty

My family and some of Grace's and Tom's friends met at the church to decorate. Trent showed up, too. He had bruises on his face and he'd broken a couple of fingers, so he had some splints on one hand. Of course, I saw the other guy, so I know he was a little dented up himself after Trent hammered him with that big stick a couple of times.

I cried when I saw him. Yeah, I'm an emotional wreck lately, anyway, but somehow he didn't look this banged up last night. Maybe because the alley was dark. I wasn't sobbing, but tears fell. I had to apologize to him.

"Trent, I'm sorry that you got hurt on my account."

"I'm not," he said.

That took me a little by surprise. "You're not?" I asked.

"Nope. It's what it took to stall that freak until the police arrived, so I'm glad it was me and not you that got hurt."

That made me cry harder. He put his good arm around me. "It's okay, Ann." I didn't even mind that he used that nickname. I barely noticed it. Okay, I noticed it, but I didn't hold it against him, even though the way he smiled I could tell he was teasing. He kissed me on the cheek.

"Brooke and I broke up," he blurted out.

"What? Why? You don't look that bad. Is it because you helped me? That woman is heartless!" I'd always figured she'd do something like that to him someday.

"I broke up with her, Annika," he said quietly.

"Why?"

"Because I'm not in love with her."

"You've dated all this time, and you aren't even in love with her? How heartless!"

He laughed. "I don't think she's that heartbroken. Really it was mutual."

"I saw you two kissing at the movie theater!" More blurting, this was the day for it.

"Oh, did you? Okay, how many of these guys you dated did you kiss?"

"Actually, only Ben, and you saw how that turned out. Oh, and Jonah, but that was a one-way kiss." I touched one of Trent's bruises. He winced. "You should've iced that."

"Brooke and I were never meant to be, and we both knew it, so we called it a day. It was as simple as that."

I don't know if I believe that explanation, but he had to leave then to pick up his tux. It doesn't matter that they're not dating anyway. What's that got to do with me? He still invaded my privacy in a way no one had before and didn't even seem to feel remorse for doing it. I don't need friends like that. He'll be at all of these events, though. Since he saved my life, I'll be civil to him, but that's all.

* * *

Well, at first I thought Trent was confused about the meaning of "rehearsal." It wasn't a dress rehearsal of course, but he showed up in his tuxedo! When I saw him come in, I was sure that Grace would have a conniption. He was going to be all wrinkled and spill food on the suit for sure at the rehearsal dinner. I didn't look bad myself, wearing a little black dress, but it wasn't my bridesmaid dress, of course.

Well, I looked at Grace, and she didn't seem hysterical at all. In fact, she seemed calmer than she's been all month. She and Tom were up talking to the people in the string ensemble, but when Trent walked in, they stopped to watch him.

He strode right up to me, dropped to one knee, pulled out an engagement ring, grabbed one of my hands with his good hand, and said, "Will you marry me, Annika?"

Shocked is not a strong enough word to describe what I felt at that moment. "Wh-why would you ask me to marry you?" Probably not the response he was expecting.

"I love you."

"No, you don't."

"Yes, I love you."

"You're just on the rebound from Brooke!"

"No, I dated her on the rebound from you."

"You couldn't rebound from me. We never dated..."

"...because you were married to your career."

"I wouldn't say I was married to it..." I began.

"Stop arguing. Are you going to marry me or not?" he said.

"You're probably just doing this to get me to do your taxes for free. I won't, by the way; they're a mess."

"Well, Turbo Tax is really complicated..."

I couldn't believe this! I started to leave. I almost got away, too, because he was still on the floor and had only the one good arm. He hung on, though.

"Trent, we're just friends. We get Chinese together."

"Okay, do you want to get Chinese with me for the rest of our life?"

That just sounded stupid. I laughed. He wasn't laughing. In fact, I think he was getting tired of kneeling on the floor. No doubt he was in pain. That's when I noticed that everyone had crowded around and was listening. It was getting embarrassing. I brought out the big guns.

"What about the letter?" I said.

"What about it?"

"You invaded my privacy!"

"I looked at it like scouting out the competition."

"I wrote that letter!"

"I know. I didn't know that at first. Anyway, you left it lying around. If you don't want someone to read something, don't leave it lying around. We shouldn't have secrets, anyway."

I immediately thought of this blog. No way I would ever tell him about this.

"I know about the blog, too," he said.

I gasped. "How?"

"Grace told me."

Grace was standing there with that sly smile of hers. She thinks she knows everything.

"I'm Annikawhatareyouthinking," he said.

I gasped again. "What?"

"Everyone you know has been reading your blog all along and commenting. How do you think I knew where to find you all those times?"

I looked around at my family standing there, grinning broadly. I closed my eyes. Have you ever wished to simply dematerialize like you were on Star Trek and reappear somewhere else? If only I could say "Beam me anywhere, Scotty..."

"Annika?"

I opened my eyes. Trent was still on the floor. I tugged at his hand. "Get up!" I whispered.

"I will as soon as you answer me."

I wish I could tell you I said something sophisticated or even said I needed to think about it. But looking into those eyes that I'd been looking into for so long, knowing that he belonged to someone else, sure that he'd never thought of me in that way for one second even if he didn't belong to someone else. After dating fifty guys while the one I wanted showed up at my door regularly seeing me as nothing more than a friend to share pot stickers with. Denying what I felt for him even anonymously (I thought) on my blog because I knew I didn't stand a chance...

"Sure," I said smiling.

* * *

I'm not there yet in feeling what I'd call brotherly love for Tom, but I can tolerate him now since I heard about his part in the conspiracy to get Trent and me together. Turns out everyone agreed from the start that they'd only set me up with guys that I'd never be interested in, guys I was totally incompatible with. Nice. Their plan was that I'd compare these guys to Trent and realize I loved him.

Grace said that all along she could tell Trent and Brooke weren't meant to be together. Grace's plan for Trent was to make him jealous when I dated all those guys.

Unfortunately, they didn't plan on Ben the stalker. Unknowingly, though, he contributed to their plan by scaring me, which ultimately made Trent look even better and of course gave Trent a chance to insert himself into the "catch Annika's stalker" experience.

I have a devious family. Of course, they didn't intend for my coworkers and friends to get involved. It worried them at first, because it might interfere with their plans. They finally figured if I met a great guy that way, then it was God's will.

Kind of like Grace and Tom who met by accident because Nadine and I visited the fitness center. At first I thought it was just a case of love is blind. Actually love wasn't blind; I was, in more ways than one. Maybe someday I'll decide theirs is a match made in heaven. Either way, Lam is part of it, too. He's meant to be included in their family. I feel it in my bones.

This morning Lam must not have approved of the food I bought him. I heard some scraping noises in the kitchen. I went in and caught him knocking his bowl around like a hockey puck. Food was flying. When he saw me he stopped and nonchalantly walked away. Tom deserves this cat.

The day of the wedding dawned bright and clear. Pretty soon, though, it clouded up and started to rain.

"Rain on your wedding day is lucky," Mom said to Grace who was standing at the window watching the downpour.

"They only say that to try to make you feel better because it rained and ruined your wedding day."

"Nah, it's not ruined. It'll be fine," I said.

Grace smiled at me. "You're in a wonderful mood," she said smugly.

"Now Grace, don't take all the credit for Annika and Trent getting together," Mom said.

Grace looked pensive. "I think I should. Trent and Annika never would have gotten together without me. They'd been going on for years pretending to be friends because neither would admit to the other one that they were in love."

"I know, dear, but we must always leave room for the Lord to work. Really our part is so small. You're saying it was all you, Grace," she said.

"Oh, everyone else helped somewhat, although it was my idea. Ultimately, I did leave it in God's hands. I prayed over and over, 'Father give Annika some sense and show her she's in love.' He finally did. He just used me to do it," and off she went to get ready.

Wouldn't it be great if I could say that Grace's wedding day went off without a hitch? It did stop raining in time and dried up nicely, and there was a rainbow over the church. The photographer got a beautiful picture of it.

I wish I could tell you that Aunt Tilly was in her right mind and didn't dance the Watusi center stage, or that Aunt Trudy wasn't ostracized by everyone. Or that all of Trent's bruises were healed and didn't show in the wedding photos.

No, I can't say any of that, but it was a beautiful wedding. I do think it was the most romantic wedding so far. And I don't know what they did to make this cake taste so fantastic, but I've got to say, it was the best wedding cake I've ever had.